Listen to Me

Listen to Me

Hannah Pittard

Houghton Mifflin Harcourt

BOSTON   NEW YORK

2016

www.hmhco.com

Library of Congress Cataloging-in-Publication Data
Pittard, Hannah.
Listen to me / Hannah Pittard.
pages ; cm
ISBN 978-0-544-71444-1 (hardcover) — ISBN 978-0-544-71523-3 (ebook)
I. Title.
PS3616.I8845L58 2016
813'.6 — dc23
2015020513

Book design by Rachel Newborn

Printed in the United States of America
DOC 10 9 8 7 6 5 4 3 2 1

For Andrew, without whom this story wouldn't exist

Listen to me and I will speak: but first swear, by word and hand, that you will keep me safe with all your heart.

—HOMER, *THE ILIAD*

auto |

      informal

      n. a motor car.

ORIGIN late 19th cent.: abbreviation of AUTOMOBILE.

auto- |

      comb. form

      self: *autoanalysis*

      · one's own: *autobiography*

      · by oneself: *automatic*

      · by itself: *automaton*

ORIGIN from Greek: *autos* **'self.'**

Listen to Me

1

They were on the road later than they intended. They'd wanted to make Indianapolis by noon, but they overslept. Mark offered to walk the dog while Maggie packed up the car. He'd wanted her to pack up the car the night before, but Maggie said it was nuts to leave a car full of luggage on a side street in Chicago.

"Every time," she'd said. "We go through this every time."

"You worry too much," he said.

"Maybe you don't worry enough."

It was dark by the time they'd had this argument and late, which meant Maggie had already won.

And so, in the morning, it was Mark — as promised — who took the dog out so that Maggie could arrange the car. But downstairs, in the private entrance to their apartment (*Private entrance!* It had taken forever, but three years ago they'd finally found the perfect apartment with its own perfectly private entrance, which they didn't have to share with a single other person, a fact that, to this day, continued to bring Maggie sharp, if fleeting, joy) was the week's recycling, just sitting there at the bottom of the stairs. Mark swore he'd taken it out.

Clearly, he hadn't.

She put down the luggage and was about to pick up the bin to do the job herself when she saw it: a pink-gold length of foil peeking up from beneath a newspaper. She pushed the paper aside.

Her heart sank — exactly what she thought: the foil was attached to an empty bottle of champagne. Her bottle of champagne. Hers and Mark's, from their last anniversary. She'd been saving it. For what, she didn't know. But she'd liked looking at it every now and then where she'd stashed it above the refrigerator next to the cookbooks. True, it had been a while since she'd taken any real note of the thing. Even so. It made her sad to think he'd thrown it out without ceremony, which was an overly sentimental concern — did an empty bottle truly merit ceremony? — but what was she going to do? Suddenly become a different person?

According to the Enneagram, which she'd taken on the recommendation of her therapist — *former* therapist, Maggie had stopped seeing her three weeks ago — everyone emerged from childhood with a basic personality type. Maggie's was Loyalist. Think: committed, hard-working, reliable. Also according to the Enneagram (she'd done some recent reading on her own), people didn't change from their basic type. Instead, throughout their lives, they vacillated between nine different levels within their type, the healthiest being a One.

Lately, Maggie was about an Eight. Think: paranoia, hysteria, irrational behavior. Her goal, by the end of the summer, was to be back at her usual Three or Four. There wasn't an overnight solution.

She picked up the bottle. Even empty, its weight was significant. Mark had splurged because they could. Because life was good and on what else were they going to spend their money?

"There are no luggage racks on hearses," they sometimes said to one another. "Spend it if you've got it." Mostly they were joking — they never spent beyond their means. But it was only just the two of them. They had no children's educations to consider, and so why not enjoy an extravagance every once in a while?

She tore off a sliver of the pink foil — the tiniest of keepsakes! — then slipped it into her back pocket. Perhaps Mark was testing her, measuring her steadiness by relieving her of an ultimately trivial trinket. Yet he'd been so patient these last nine months, so generous with his affection — kissing her shoulder before clearing the table, squeezing her hand before falling asleep. Sure, they'd quarreled about the luggage and maybe the last three weeks had been more strained than usual, but quarrels, as Maggie and her former therapist had discussed, were the latticework of relationships. They were the branches — interlacing the pattern, strengthening the structure — that sheltered them and kept them together.

She put the bottle back in the bin, right at the very top. She didn't need to say a thing about it. She would pass his test with flying colors.

Mark and Gerome were crossing the street when she emerged from the front door.

"What are you doing?" said Mark.

"The recycling," she said. She held up the bin. "You didn't take it out."

She watched his eyes; they didn't acknowledge the bottle.

"Gerome didn't do anything," Mark said.

Maggie looked down at Gerome, who was looking up at her and wagging his tail. He sneezed.

"What do you mean?" she said.

"He didn't go."

"He always goes."

Gerome was still wagging his tail.

"You're driving him crazy with the recycling." Mark held out his hands to take it.

"You don't do it right," she said.

"If I chuck it all at once or put it in piece by piece doesn't matter. It all goes to the same place, whether it's broken or not."

Maggie shrugged. He was right. She knew he was right. She wasn't an idiot, but there was something so gloomy about Mark carelessly hurling it all away. Just as there was something equally gloomy about watching the homeless man who walked their alley take off his gloves one finger at a time before searching the recycling for refundable bottles. It was silly to think their bottles and cans contributed anything significant to the man's well-being, but she couldn't help it. The thought of him fingering broken bits of glass made her heart ache. Of course, she hadn't actually seen anyone going through the trash since autumn, as she hadn't taken out the recycling since her mugging, and yet here she was still thinking about it, and here it was filling her afresh with sadness, a condition both new and not new.

For nine months, the sadness had been constant — a heavy, dull fog lingering greedily about the nape of her neck. She was aware of it in the morning when she woke, in the afternoon when she worked, in the evening when she scoured the Internet, seeking out the most miserable stories of human woe.

When Mark came home from teaching, he'd sometimes find her in front of the computer. He would ask, "What are you doing?" And she'd say, "Reading the Internet. Reading about this girl who just died. Reading about this boy who was killed. Reading about this teenager who kidnapped a jogger and took her body apart limb by limb." He had been so devoted the first few months after the incident in the alley, when the sadness was pushing down around her. He would close the computer, take her hand, lead her

4

to the living room, and read aloud to her. He had a magnificent reading voice. Sometimes he chose a bit of poetry. Sometimes history or philosophy. They both liked Augustine and stories of war. Yeats was also a favorite. Mark would occasionally ask about her therapy. The sadness had begun to lift. The appointments had been helping. She stopped seeking out those awful news articles and started reading about other Loyalists online, about their own struggles with fear and personal insecurity. Maggie had felt herself returning. She'd felt the fog lightening, her levels stabilizing. Things with Mark were as good as ever.

But then, just three weeks ago — out of nowhere and with no warning whatsoever — the police appeared. They showed up at the front door of the apartment with pictures of a body, a coed who lived just down the street. They presented them to Maggie. Why had they let her see them? She hadn't understood then and still didn't now. They also presented photos of a man, the one responsible for the coed. *Was it the same man?* they wanted to know. Was it the man who'd struck Maggie with the butt of a gun and left her for dead not two blocks from where she lived?

For several hours, they pored over the photographs together and sifted through the evidence. What they discovered was that it was *not* the same man. Maggie had been as disappointed and relieved as the police by this revelation. But the coed was someone she knew. Not as a friend, of course. Not even by name — at least not before the news coverage. But she'd known the girl's dog, a Chihuahua mix called Ginger. She'd said hello countless times as they crossed paths on the sidewalk — Maggie heading toward the dog park, Ginger and the coed coming from.

By the time Mark got home from work on the night of the cops' visit, the damage was done. The photos had already been taken out of the manila envelope, already placed one by one on the kitchen table in front of Maggie, who was sitting — when

Mark walked in — across from the detectives, her hand to her mouth, unable and unwilling to look away.

The next day, Maggie indefinitely suspended sessions with her therapist. She cut back on hours at the veterinary clinic, giving many of her regular and favorite pets to her colleagues. It was her clinic, she reasoned, and she could do as she pleased. Mark had been trying so hard — those kisses, those hand squeezes — to be patient. But Maggie, freshly fanatic and disturbed beyond language at the pictures of the coed, dedicated herself anew to her sadness, to the Internet, to any story that might confirm her suspicions of the world, of the turbulent state of humanity.

Consequently, for the past three weeks, when Mark came home from work and found Maggie sitting at the kitchen table — the overhead lights turned off, the white hue of the computer screen illuminating her face — instead of taking her hand and shutting the laptop, he turned away and walked into any other room in the apartment than the one she was in.

What Mark didn't understand — what the Enneagram did, however, and what her therapist might have if Maggie had been as forthcoming as expected — was that even if the Internet had been taken away, she'd still have had her imagination. Just then, for instance, looking at the champagne that the two of them had opened with such relish in honor of their anniversary, she couldn't help also thinking of the homeless man taking off his gloves, going through the recycling, and discovering the bottle that would have broken upon impact — if she were to let Mark take it to the back, where he would dump the bin without any further consideration — into shards.

"I can do it," said Maggie. "I can empty the bin by myself."

"Fine."

Mark started toward the front door.

"What are you doing?" she said.

6

"Going inside. Eating breakfast."

"What about Gerome?"

Mark widened his eyes like he had no clue what she was talking about.

"He has to do something," Maggie said. "Or we'll be stopping in Gary."

Mark threw up his hands, unintentionally yanking Gerome's neck. "Why would it be *Gary*?" he said. Gerome grunted. "Why wouldn't it be Hyde Park? Or Indianapolis?"

"Give me his leash," she said. "You're hurting him."

"If he doesn't go now, then we'll die in Gary? Is that what you're imagining?"

In fact, that *was* what she was imagining. But she hated the way he made it sound. He made it sound so ridiculous, like it was a complete impossibility. And, yes, obviously it was incredibly unlikely that Gerome would suddenly have to go just as they were passing Gary and even more unlikely that they'd pull off at some abandoned exit. But if it did happen that way — if it did, which it technically could, because it wasn't like they were talking about actually unfeasible things here (like time travel or pigs flying) — if it did happen, then Maggie would definitely be the one to walk him since Mark would be sulking and because Gerome never went to the bathroom with Mark when he was sulking because he, Gerome, could sense frustration and it made him nervous. So it would be Maggie walking the dog on some street lined with tenements, and there would be no witnesses, and it would, quite matter-of-factly, be the ideal set of circumstances if, for instance, there were a carjacker lurking or a murderer or a rapist or one of those misfits in a ski mask. And, yes, obviously all this sounded crazy — especially the way Mark had suggested it — but it's not like it wasn't possible. It's not like there weren't carjackers and murderers and rapists and masked nut jobs lurking at all those quiet exits off the tollway. Maggie had been reading the articles. Four women last month. The month before, five. And just three weeks ago, the coed, practically a neighbor. It was an epidemic. That's what troubled her. There wasn't simply one man out there. There were hundreds. Thousands. And they were waiting, just waiting for the right opportunity. All she had to do was open her laptop and there was another story.

"Here," Mark said. "Fine." He held out his hand. She juggled the recycling and took the leash.

Gerome looked back and forth between them.

"Will you at least put the bags in the trunk?" Maggie said. "I'll arrange them. You don't need to arrange them. Just put them in the trunk."

She started toward the back of the building, where the dumpsters were. But then she stopped. Goose bumps traveled the length of both arms. She turned back. Mark was standing there, as she knew he would be, watching her with a blank expression. If only he would smile; give a wink or a shrug even, as if to say, "We're okay. This is a blip. A dwarf-sized blip. Just another branch, another piece of the lattice ever strengthening our shelter." But he didn't.

Who was he thinking about? Was it one of his students? Was it a colleague? Maggie couldn't be sure, but recently — only very recently — she'd begun to suspect he might be thinking of someone else.

"So you know," she said. "I want him to go now so we don't have to stop until we need gas or lunch. I don't want to lose any more time than we already have."

Mark shook his head.

Their apartment — perfect apartment! — was above a coffee shop, which meant there were four people watching them at that exact moment. There were always at least four people sit-

8

ting at the counter, drinking their drinks, staring out at the world, watching.

"I don't care, Maggie." His tone was unfamiliar, and she disliked the way he'd said her name — as if she were a child who'd forgotten something important, as if she were clueless and ought, therefore, to be pitied.

"It's not that big a deal," he said. Then he turned around and walked inside.

2

Things hadn't always been this way between Mark and Maggie. A decade ago, when they were still in DC, still finishing up with grad school, they'd been the envy of their friends. They were never anything so drab as picture-perfect: there were fights — certainly, certainly — and disappointments. But they'd found in each other a wave, a vibe, a shared view of their interconnection with the universe.

It was early autumn when they met, at a party hosted by Georgetown's History Department and held — of all places — on a Potomac riverboat cruise. Mark had only agreed to attend because he knew the boat would remain docked. He could leave whenever he wanted. Six years into his graduate program, he was listless. In the company of other academics, he found himself bored by their inanities and the way they tended to speak more than listen. His plan that night had been to stay only for a beer or two, maybe a shake of hands with the incoming grad students — enough to show he wasn't aloof — then head off to the Tabard Inn, where he would have a late dinner and continue a recent flirtation with a bartender from Poland. She couldn't mix a drink, but she could pour gin over ice and she spoke with an accent that had caused Mark more than once to clutch his chest in sweet agony and say, "Hand to god. Your voice hurts me to my heart."

Georgetown hadn't secured the entirety of the boat — already budgets were tightening — and so a second party was also being hosted that night by a different school, which was how it happened that Mark caught Maggie's eye. Complete serendipity. She was in her final year of the veterinary program at Howard University. She was remarkably tall and, that night, dressed in a sort of Annie Hall get-up that was several decades too late, but what initially attracted Mark to Maggie — what caused him to introduce himself in the first place — was an off-kilter gap between her two front teeth, which she exposed — seemingly without embarrassment — whenever she laughed. He assumed she'd been raised either in extreme poverty or extreme wealth.

What he liked best about getting together with Maggie those first few months of dating was the way she would — in public or private — seek out direct eye contact. At parties, at dinner, stretching in the park after a run together, he would sometimes find her watching him, which in turn would lead to him watching her, and the two of them might continue to watch each other, no words spoken at all. There was something animal about Maggie, and it made Mark feel there was something animal about him — a sensation he'd never before known to crave. She was as different as could be from his cohort at school.

Maggie, it turned out, was from a family that was neither outrageously advantaged nor incredibly poor. Instead, hers was a lower-middle-class childhood — "more lower than middle," she liked to say — in the "upper middle of America" (Minnesota), where she'd been raised by a "brilliant but hateful" woman and a "handsome but unintelligent" man. Her older brother was an alcoholic who'd been given the little attention her parents could muster. Maggie was the daughter they hadn't planned on and, as such, the one who received primary blame for any money woes the family might encounter. "And we were always encountering money woes," she said. "But it's not as though we had nothing."

What was a wonder to Mark — a gift really — was the way that Maggie, rather than making him feel ashamed or embarrassed by his own privilege and upbringing, instead made him feel proud, lucky. She was always asking questions about his parents, always wanting to know more about his evening routines as a child — dinner at the table, followed by a walk in the woods with his parents, followed by reading aloud in front of the fire. Never before Maggie had he enjoyed sharing these stories, fearing always that he would be ridiculed and that his childhood might be deemed precious or out-of-touch.

And, yes, obviously those were the early days of courtship, and early days of any relationship mellow out, soften, dilute themselves into something more ordinary, less extreme, more ubiquitously accessible. Their relationship was no different than others in this regard, except that between them they retained a sincere fondness, a genuine gratefulness that the other existed and continued to exist.

But ever since that college girl's death and, subsequently, the visit from the cops, Maggie had been spending most of her time at home and in a flannel robe. Mark had no idea where she'd even gotten the thing. He only knew that one day, about two weeks ago, he'd come home from work and she was wearing it. One of those plaid L.L.Bean jobs. At first it was a joke. Or Mark thought it was a joke, or at the very least something to joke about. Then one day — a week ago max — he'd been parking the car and there was Maggie, walking down the other side of the street with Gerome. She was wearing the robe. It was afternoon. It was daylight. Mark had a sudden sinking feeling that he was married to a loser.

Maggie had an excuse for her behavior, but it was getting old. It was getting old in part because she'd been getting better. The symptoms now felt disproportionate to the cause. Like, for instance, Patricia Hatchett, who was also in the History Department, had lost a baby last year, and Mark wasn't the only one to notice that she looked better these days than ever. He'd heard she was considering a run for chair, for Christ's sake. It embarrassed Mark that his wife had become a completely different person just because she'd been mugged. Strike that — because someone they didn't even know had been murdered. But what was becoming more and more apparent — and this wasn't a happy or an easy realization — was that Mark was spending his life with one of the world's weaklings: the type of person who gets diagnosed with cancer and, instead of going outside and taking on life, gets in bed and waits for the inevitable. He'd expected more from Maggie. My god, he'd expected so much more!

How the mugging happened — what Maggie told Mark — went like this: she'd gotten off the Red Line at Berwyn. Same stop as always. It was getting dark but it wasn't late. She crossed Broadway and started into the neighborhood. A man was waiting at the first alley. He asked for change. She ignored him, kept walking. He followed. It was their neighborhood — *their* neighborhood: middle-upper class, lots of grass! — she didn't think anything of the fact that he was following her. She was three blocks from Clark Street. Three blocks from the coffee shop and their apartment and the dinner that Mark had made for them. By the next alley, though, the man had caught up to her. "Hey," he said. He tapped her on the shoulder. Not even this had set off bells that she was dealing with anything more than a simple panhandler, a meager beggar. "The purse," he said. He pointed to her bag. Her wallet and computer were inside. She laughed. "No way, dude," she said. "Sorry." She turned to walk away.

She claimed she didn't originally see the gun, but later — after a young couple had found her and called the cops and taken her to the emergency room — when they showed her photos of the bruise on the back of her neck, of the perfect outline of the butt of a gun, she said the gun had become a part of the memory. Whether it was a trick of the imagination or a real recollection had been jogged somehow, she didn't know. But ever since seeing the photos, she remembered the gun.

Not too long ago, as the winter yielded to spring, she'd gotten to the point where she was making jokes about the whole thing. She'd been fucking adorable with the story. Like, okay, at a dinner party five weeks ago — *five weeks ago!* — she'd been the belle of the ball. She told the anecdote three, maybe four times. She was a hit. A trouper. A riot. They all loved the way she'd said, "No way, dude." Nadeem Gnechik had stopped Mark in the hallway the next day and said, "Your wife's a goddamn battle-ax." They shared a laugh and Mark thought to himself, *Yes.* He thought, *A battle-ax — my wife.* He thought, *I'm a goddamn lucky man.*

But then, with the arrival of those cops and their photos, out came the flannel robe.

Last week he found two bottles of mace in the dog-walking drawer and an application for a concealed carry permit. He'd torn the paper up and pushed it to the bottom of the trash.

Just three mornings ago, on her side of the bed, he discovered a string between the mattress and the box spring. When he pulled the string, he was surprised — surprised? No, try *astonished* — to find it was attached to a small switchblade.

When she got home from the clinic that night — the first shift she'd taken since the detectives — he pointed at the switchblade, which he'd set on the middle of the kitchen table, and said, "What the fuck, Maggie? What the fuck is this?"

She'd shrugged. "It's a knife," she said. Gerome was crazy-eighting around her legs.

"I know it's a knife," he said. What alarmed him most was how dismissive she was, how suddenly calm.

"I could have died," she said. She moved for the knife. Mark grabbed it before she could. "I could be dead right now."

"Is this about the college girl?"

"Right now," she said, "you could be a widower."

"It wasn't even the same man," he said.

"It could have been."

Mark shook his head. What she was saying was crazy. What she was saying was downright lunatic. "But you're not dead. You're here. You're right here."

"But what if I weren't?" she said. "What if I weren't here?"

When he told her no more knives, when he told her he drew the line at weapons in the bedroom, she shrugged again. "If you don't give it back, I'll just buy another one. Play it how you want." It was maddening that she refused him the discussion.

Normal people didn't waste their days reading about other people's misfortunes. Normal people didn't take a gross sort of pleasure in keeping up with local crime statistics. Normal people didn't walk the dog in a robe. Normal people didn't act like Maggie.

The semester would be over in a few weeks, at which point the two of them would make their annual drive east for a couple months at Mark's parents' farm. His hope was to finish several chapters of his latest manuscript, a history of anonymity, which he believed — if pulled off correctly — might put him on the academic map in a major way. But Mark didn't think he could wait

16

another few weeks to make the drive. He was frightened by what Maggie was capable of. He'd found the mace. He'd found the application for a gun and that terrifyingly sharp little switchblade. But what might she bring home next? What might already be hidden that he hadn't yet found?

Mark understood — a sort of hammer-to-the-skull-type realization, as Maggie walked out of the kitchen, leaving him alone with the knife and its distressing string attachment — that his wife must be removed from the city immediately. Distance needed to be created between Maggie and her desire for blades, guns, and even the Internet. A return to nature — to Wordsworth's meadow, grove, and stream — was essential for them both.

When Mark went out with the dog that night, he called his mother.

"We're coming this weekend," he said.

In the background, he could hear his father knocking about loudly with the evening's dishes.

"Is it June already?" his mother said. "Am I losing my mind?" Then, before Mark could answer, she said to his father, "Mark says they're coming this weekend." Then, after a pause, she said to Mark, "Your father wants to know about classes."

"We're going into finals," he said. "I'll get a grad student to administer them. It's fine."

There was another back-and-forth between his parents, along with more clanging and clattering of pots and pans. His mother again: "Your father says that's cheating the students." Mark's father was a retired professor. He'd been a trailblazer in the field of eco studies and was now emeritus faculty at the University of Virginia, something that filled Mark with equal parts satisfaction and envy. It occasionally disappointed him — thinking he'd never have a son of his own who might eventually entertain such complicated feelings about him.

"Remind him I have tenure," Mark said. "Is the cabin ready?"

"It's always ready."

Mark had expected pushback from Maggie when he told her, later that night, of his decision.

Instead, she looked up from her laptop and said, "I like this on you." She'd changed from jeans into loose-fitting sweatshorts and was sitting cross-legged in bed, on top of the covers. Wedged beneath her thigh was a copy of that test she'd taken. It was open to a dog-eared page. Several answers had pencil annotations beside them.

"You like what on me?" Mark unhooked Gerome's leash, and the dog went instantly to Maggie, hopping up and circling into place at the foot of their bed.

"Spontaneity."

He wondered if she was fucking with him.

Three days later and Lake Shore Drive, like they both knew it would be, was a mess.

By the time Gerome had done everything he needed to do and by the time the car was packed, the apartment locked up, the trash and recycling taken out, they were practically begging to coincide with the weekend rush hour. And they did.

"Fuck," said Mark. The traffic came to a standstill at Belmont. They'd gone only three miles. "Fuck. Fuck."

Gerome stood up in the backseat.

"When you're tense," said Maggie, "it makes him tense. Dogs are mirrors of their owners."

She turned around in her seat and tried to coax Gerome into sitting, but he whined and stayed standing.

"I can't see," said Mark. "If he's like that, I can't see anything out the back."

"We're not moving," she said. "When we start moving, he'll sit down."

A car nearby honked. Another followed suit. Gerome whined again.

"We won't be there until after midnight," said Mark. "Plus we lose an hour. Fuck."

Maggie was still jackknifed in her seat, trying to calm the dog. "We'll make it," she said. "We always do."

Gerome reluctantly curled himself into a ball.

"We can get a hotel," said Mark, "if we have to."

"Gerome can't handle a hotel," she said. "You know that."

"He's a dog. He'll handle what we tell him to."

In fact, Gerome was a disaster in hotels, and Mark knew it. The one time they'd forgotten the sound machine — an attempt at a last-minute romantic getaway to Nashville last year, pre-mugging — they'd had to leave the shower running and the television on all night. Mark had tried repeatedly to initiate sex, but Maggie — normally so keen, still, after all these years — was too focused on the dog's discomfort to focus on him. So they'd turned on the shower *and* the television because it was the only way Gerome would shut up. In the morning they drove back to Chicago, overtired and newly distant. But Mark, as a point of pride, liked to assume that the last time would be, well, the last time. He liked to assume the next time would be better. That's the kind of guy he was — always looking ahead, always looking up, which was what he'd been trying to do with Maggie. But she was making it hard. The world — those cops, that college girl, the media itself — was conspiring against him.

A few miles east of where Mark and Maggie's car was currently at a standstill — 925 feet below the surface — was the deepest point of Lake Michigan. At the bottom of the lake, pitch-black, there exists a vast world of hidden networks and drowned river channels, evidence of a catastrophic overflow from Superior into Michigan during the Holocene times, which is to say the geological epoch some 11,700 years BP, which is to say *before present,* which is also to say *before physics,* which is the time *before* nuclear testing, which is the time *after* which carbon isotopes in the atmosphere were artificially altered, rendering time — its accurate apprehension — untrustworthy.

Maggie scratched the dog's head and turned forward. "We won't need a hotel," she said. "I promise." She adjusted the a/c vent, closed her eyes, and angled her face so that the current pushed her hair away from her forehead. "Mmm," she said, suddenly so calm, so Zen.

It was like —

It was like sometimes — these last three weeks especially — he was living with a stranger. Sometimes, just looking at her, it was like he didn't recognize a single thing about his wife.

3

They cleared all three exits for Gary without saying a word. Mark pretended he didn't even notice. Maggie stared out the window as the city passed below them. Gary wasn't just a place to die. It was, as far as she was concerned, a place to be killed. It was a place to hate your life, a place to sweat your day away in an attic apartment while you listened to dogs fight to death in the alley. It was in Gary that a shallow grave had been discovered just that spring. The body belonged to a fifteen-year-old boy. He weighed less than fifty pounds. She'd read all about it: his parents had kept him outside, in a cage. Bad things happened in Gary.

Gerome was snoring. He had maneuvered his body so that his forearms and head were stretched onto the armrest between the front seats. It couldn't have been comfortable, but he was only ever truly relaxed when he was touching one or both of them. Maggie ran a finger over his nose leather. Cold and wet. Gerome was a mix, which meant he was a healthy dog. When her clients asked, she always recommended mutts. Pure breeds helped the clinic's bank account, sure, but that was it. Pure breeds — and she wasn't shy about saying so — pure breeds were accidents waiting to happen. Boston terriers? All of them were brachycephalics, and half were born with luxating patellas. Bernese mountain dogs? Most were dead by five. Great Danes? With those hips? Don't get her started.

Lake Shore had added an extra hour, but once they hit 90/94, they were essentially traffic-free. Just them and the big rigs, and they were actively making good time. If they stopped only when they needed gas, there was a chance they could still make the Blue Ridge Parkway by midnight. It was possible they wouldn't have to get a hotel. They'd wake up in Virginia to green grass and full forests. Maggie and Gerome could go for their first official farm run of summer.

They'd only just taken the exit off 90 for 65, a hundred and some miles outside Chicago, but Mark was in a visibly better mood. He'd turned on the radio, and every few minutes he flipped through the channels. Even though Mark couldn't find talk radio, he seemed happy. The fifty-mile stretch of turbines always calmed him down.

"How many do you think there are?" Maggie hadn't intended to ask the question aloud, but it was a relief to break their silence.

"More than six hundred," said Mark.

She tried counting the number of turbines in a single row. She gave up at ten.

"When it's completed," Mark said, "they say it'll be the largest in the world."

"They must be — what? — two hundred feet tall?"

"Closer to three hundred," he said.

Maggie moved nearer to her window and gazed up at the one they were passing.

"They look like gods," she said. "Enormous three-armed gods." She leaned back in her seat.

On the west side of 65, the windmills' blades were still. To the east, they were turning at full speed. "You could explain it to me a million times — harnessing wind power — and it would never make sense. Try to imagine the first person, standing in some storm, getting rocked about by the wind, thinking, *I can work with this*."

"His name was James Blyth."

"How on earth do you know that?"

"A professor in Glasgow. Late nineteenth century."

"Your father quizzed you as a child."

"Of course he did."

"Instead of playing in the snow, you were sitting in front of a chalkboard."

"Yep."

"You poor thing." It was an act, of course, and one they both enjoyed. Mark's childhood, as Maggie well knew and admired, had been spent almost entirely outdoors. He'd been given books obviously. His parents had monitored his evening reading habits closely, but during the day he'd been encouraged to engage with the wilderness. Before Mark turned ten, he'd built a canoe with his father. Before high school, he'd built another on his own. The second one was mounted, family-crest-like, on the wall of the guest cabin on his parents' farm, high above the wood-burning fireplace.

They were both still in grad school when Mark first took Maggie to his parents' farm. "They're eccentric," he'd said more than once on the drive from DC. They'd been talking recently about moving in with one another, though they hadn't yet talked about rings. "My mother can be competitive," he said. "Plus you're a knockout, so Robert will be overly attentive, which means Gwen might act out. Also, she's going through an astrology phase, so fair warning."

In fact, when Mark and Maggie arrived, Gwen had been so

welcoming, so immediately receptive, that Maggie had wondered briefly at his capacity for accuracy. But as the night wore on — and after several bottles of wine had been opened and poured — Maggie did begin to see glimpses of the so-called eccentricities. For starters, at midnight, when she was so tired she nearly fell asleep on the couch, instead of being allowed to go immediately to bed, she was walked by Gwen into Gwen and Robert's bedroom.

"Come, dear heart," his mother had said. "I want to show you something."

Maggie tried to linger in the doorway — she'd rarely stepped foot into her own parents' room — but Gwen took her hand and pulled her to the bed. "Sit here," she said.

Maggie did as told, though she felt her presence in their bedroom was inappropriate; she couldn't say why. She longed to be in the company of Mark and Robert; longed to be in a common living space, where meetings between strangers were customary and formal.

What Gwen showed Maggie that night was a deck of Tarot cards. "Have you ever had your palms read?" asked Gwen. "I'm a newbie. I need practice, and I can only read Robert's so many times. Do you mind?"

"Oh," said Maggie. She looked at the door to the bedroom. "I'm so tired."

"This won't take long," she said. "Besides, you should always please the mother. Isn't that what they say?"

"Is it?" Maggie said.

"You're a hoot. Now let me read."

Maggie could no longer remember the cards Gwen read for her, but she remembered the way her stiffness gradually fell away. By the end of the reading, she was sitting cross-legged on Mark's parents' bed, her back against their pillows, gabbing about her life back in DC.

When Mark finally came to fetch her, it was nearly two in the morning, and any fatigue she'd felt earlier had been spirited away by Gwen's exuberance. He leaned in the doorway watching them. "You've made a little girl out of my Maggie," he said.

His mother threw a pillow at him. "I've seen her destiny," she said. "See, look. I'll show you."

As Gwen proceeded to move the cards about on the bed, lining them up and explaining them all over again now to her son, Maggie watched Mark and Mark watched Maggie. Neither of them was listening to Gwen. Their focus was singular, intense.

"The point is," said Gwen, rising suddenly, causing Maggie to bounce slightly, "it seems you've found the one. It's in the cards. Your future; your doom." She brushed her hands together as if wiping away crumbs. "Now out. The two of you. I'm old and tired. Tell your father it's time for bed."

Mark and Maggie slept that night not in his boyhood bedroom but in the guest cabin (*the guest cabin!*), its windows high and open. They pulled the mattress from the bed and centered it in the middle of the room, close to the fire, so that Maggie could take in the handiwork of Mark's handmade canoe as he told her stories of the wilderness just beyond their walls. They didn't have sex that night, but they held hands and fell asleep naked, and Maggie, in her final moment of consciousness before giving herself up to sleep, had thought, *The one. I've found the one.*

"I could drive," said Maggie. She reached over and touched Mark's leg. Gerome stretched and shifted so that his head was now weighing down her wrist, as if he could indefinitely keep her there. She moved her arm away gently. The dog sighed.

Mark scratched between Gerome's ears but didn't take his eyes off the road.

"When we need gas," he said. "I feel good right now."

"But you like to watch the windmills," she said.

He glanced over and gave her a smile. "You watch them for me," he said.

Lately, this was how it went after a squabble like the one they'd had that morning — a slow, sweet back-and-forth of trivial politesse and minor deference. They behaved like people unfamiliar with one another, people entering anew into the world of social contracts. The intimacy would return eventually. It always did. It mostly always did. But first the quiet back-and-forth.

Sometimes, since the mugging, Maggie thought they behaved like a couple who'd lost a child, the way they'd be overly kind and curiously formal with one another. There was never an apology, never any blame after one of their spats, as though the thing they couldn't mention was a dead child. And, yet, there was no dead child. It had always been just the two of them. The two of them and Gerome.

Before the mugging, their fights would invariably lead to sex. One would yell, the other would scream, but within moments there would be laughter — it was only life after all! What was there ever to be so truly angry about? — and from laughter with the two of them there was only the shortest of walks to sex. Maggie didn't suspect she and Mark were necessarily unique in their sustained chemistry so many years into their marriage. In fact, she rather liked the idea that other couples might be as frisky as they behind closed doors. But — inappropriately or not — she did take pride in their sex life, and so in the months following the mugging, she occasionally found herself pining for the energy that had once seemed a permanent fixture in their bedroom life.

In high school Maggie had gone steady with only one boy. On three separate occasions she'd thwarted his attempts to have sex. After the third attempt — they were in the backseat of his mother's station wagon; she could remember the coldness of an open magazine against her thighs — the boy had turned gloomy. "Are you a prude or something?" he'd asked, pulling back abruptly and leaning dramatically against the door. She'd answered honestly, as honestly as she could at any rate. She'd told him no, she didn't think she was. "It's just that I can't see falling in love with you," she said. "I can't picture it in my mind."

What Maggie *could* picture — not then, but these days, and somehow more vividly than ever — was the mugging. It wasn't a memory she purposely sought out; was, in fact, one that she'd gone to great lengths to sort through and move past. But in the glossiness of the photographs that those two detectives had placed before her, she'd encountered a trigger, and the trauma of her own incident — the fear she'd felt when she finally understood, the helplessness of that nanosecond between awareness and loss of consciousness — came back to her, lodging itself in the periphery of her temporal lobe. And now it was always just there — above her, over her, behind her — that awful little man and his terrible gruff voice. *Lady. Lady.*

She'd been in a good mood that night. She'd gone down to River North for a ladies' luncheon — Women in the Workplace — where she'd given a short talk on her rise to success: the necessary sacrifices, the powerful rewards. She'd stayed longer than she intended, mingling with guests, drinking champagne. By the time she phoned Mark, he'd already left campus and was headed home. "I went by the store," he said. "I'm making dinner. If you leave now, you'll be home just as I'm pouring the first glass of wine."

She'd walked to the Red Line at Grand with a few other women, parted ways with one-armed hugs and side kisses, then walked down to the underground platform. The train arrived almost immediately. She secured a front-facing seat by a window and passed the twenty-minute ride marveling at her reflection and its hazy little smile. She liked the sensation — the out-of-body, atmospheric quality — of being slightly buzzed while also being hurdled atop the city at fifty miles an hour. At Berwyn, she'd nearly skipped down the stairs she was feeling so boisterous, so generally good about herself and her life. (She hadn't skipped, obviously, but she'd had the feeling, which in turn had caused a youthful sensation of butterflies and inexplicable happiness. Life was just so *satisfying* sometimes.)

When, a few blocks later, a man approached her, she thought nothing of it. People were always telling her, reassuring her, that bad things happened (a) to bad people, (b) when good people behaved poorly, or (c) when any kind of person ignored obvious warning signs. She was largely inclined to agree, though she understood it was a surface-level analysis at best, one that didn't, for instance, take into account the Joseph Heller adage, which she also agreed with: *Just because you're paranoid, doesn't mean they aren't after you.* On the night it happened, she hadn't been behaving poorly and for a fact she knew that she wasn't a bad person and there'd been no credible warning signs. She'd been so naïve then, so painfully trusting. A fully developed Loyalist, a level One, would have been more vigilant. If only Gerome had been with her.

Mark's phone rang. He pulled it from his jacket pocket and handed it to Maggie. Gerome stood, stretched, then dropped down fully in the backseat.

"Who is it?" Mark said.

The fact that he was willing to hand his phone to her like that, that he didn't seem nervous there might be a name he didn't want her to see — well, it made Maggie feel foolish for suspecting him earlier that morning of thinking of someone else. It made her feel foolish for suspecting him ever. Of course there was no one else. She was his Maggie.

"If it's my mom, do you mind taking it?" he said. "If you don't want to, I completely understand." The strange Ping-Pong of over-articulated etiquette was still in effect.

Maggie looked down. It was, indeed, his mother.

"You're right," she said. "Mind reader." She answered the phone.

"Gwen," she said. "Hi. Mark's driving."

Mark nudged her and then, in a whisper, he said, "Tell her we might not be there until tomorrow."

Maggie shooed away his hand.

"Have you cleared Cincinnati?" said Gwen. "Robert and I have money on this. I think you'll have passed Cincinnati."

Robert and Gwen put money on everything. Sometimes it was funny. Sometimes it wasn't. When they put money on Mark's tenure, for instance, it was not funny at all that Robert had bet against.

"I wish," said Maggie. "I hope you didn't bet much."

"Darn," said Gwen. "Robert knew you'd get a late start."

"And how," said Maggie.

Mark turned down the radio.

"Actually," Maggie said, "Mark thinks we'll need a hotel, but I don't know. We might make up time."

"Tell her we haven't even made Indianapolis," Mark whispered.

Maggie shushed him. To Gwen, she said, "What do you think? Do you think we ought to stop if it gets too late?"

There was silence on the other end.

"Gwen? You there?"

"Yes. Sorry. Robert is saying something. Hold on."

Maggie held the phone away from her ear. Robert must have been in another room because Gwen was shouting at him and he was shouting something back.

Mark furrowed his eyebrows, as if to ask, *What gives?*

Maggie shrugged.

In front of them, a Mack truck filled with pigs veered onto the shoulder and into the rumble strip. The trailer fishtailed into the left lane, narrowly dodging the debris of a commercial tire strewn across the highway.

"Fuck," said Mark.

He tapped the brakes. Gerome sat up. Maggie put a hand on the dog's withers. The truck recovered its course.

"Shh," she said. "It's okay." Her heart was racing a little. Double tires always sounded worse on a rumble strip.

"Fuck," said Mark. "Did you see that?"

Maggie massaged Gerome's shoulder.

"Dead tire," she said.

"I know," he said. "It looked like a carcass."

"A carcass of rubber."

"Close call," he said.

"Good driving," she said.

He reached over, squeezed her thigh. She squeezed his hand. *Yes*, she thought. *See?* The intimacy always returned.

She leaned back into the seat.

"Wait," said Mark.

"What?"

"The phone."

It was on the floorboard.

"I completely forgot," she said. "I must have dropped it."

A small tinny voice was calling their names through the speaker. Maggie picked it up.

"Hi," she said. "Hi. We're here. Gwen?"

"I thought you'd had an accident," she said.

"No, no. We're here."

"You nearly gave me a heart attack."

(In fact, the amygdala, not the heart, is the seat of emotion. It is an almond-shaped region in the brain that speaks, on occasion, to that hollow muscular organ.)

Maggie said, "I don't know if you heard me —"

"Robert says to turn on the weather station. He says there are storms in Ohio and West Virginia. They're having outages. Statewide. He wants you to be safe. This is big. They're saying tornadoes. Tor-na-*does*."

Ninety-three million miles overhead, the sun was gloriously and uproariously on full display. The sky out the sunroof was bright blue. There wasn't a single cloud. Maggie gazed ahead. What was the distance of the horizon supposed to be? Two miles? Three? That couldn't be right. Indiana was so flat, so ruthlessly flat. Surely she was seeing something closer to ten miles, maybe even twenty miles into the distance, and as far as she could see, the skies were clear.

"We'll probably get a hotel," said Maggie. "It's what Mark wants."

"Men and their hotel rooms," said Gwen. "Just let us know. Love to Mark."

The line went dead.

She handed Mark his phone. "Madness," she said. "Sheer madness."

"Did she hang up on you?"

"As always."

He reached over and touched her cheek. "It's technology," he said. "It's made assholes out of all of us."

They were passing the final few rows of turbines. Maggie looked out the window again. No matter how often they made this drive, no matter how many times she scanned the tops of the towers, she'd never — not once — seen a person up there. She could make out the little doorways; identify the safety fences wrapped like toothpicks around the gearboxes. But she'd never seen a person, and it never failed to disappoint her.

To her right was the exit for Purdue University, where Mark had interviewed just after finishing his dissertation. He'd been offered the job and the school had flown them both out from DC for a weekend visit, an unsuccessful attempt to woo Mark away from the Chicago offer he already planned to accept. Maggie remembered little of Lafayette itself. Of the hotel, on the other hand . . . They'd stopped after the faculty dinner to buy beer at a nearby gas station, and Maggie, when Mark wasn't looking, sneaked a travel-pack of condoms into her purse. When Mark went to pay for the six-pack, the man behind the counter asked if he was also planning to pay for the condoms his girlfriend had stolen. Poor Mark had been caught completely off guard. Maggie, near the exit, shook her head and blushed.

The cashier held out his hand. "Either way, ma'am," he said. "Leave 'em or pay for 'em. But you can't just have 'em."

Maggie approached the cash register — she couldn't look at Mark — then removed the travel-pack and slid it across the counter.

"Looks like you were fixing to get lucky," the cashier said to Mark.

Maggie wanted to vomit she was so embarrassed.

Mark picked up the condoms, studied them, then put them squarely on top of the beer. "Looks like maybe I still am."

The cashier shrugged. "At least she knows to wrap it every time." He winked at Mark. "Good for you and for her."

Mark picked up the beer and shoved the condoms into his pocket. "She's my wife," he said.

"Sure she is." The man nodded, looked at Maggie, then grinned. "My wife's always buying condoms. Always."

Back at the hotel, they'd howled with laughter.

"He thought you were a prostitute," Mark said.

"Impossible," she said. "Look at me."

They'd rolled around on the bed a little. But out of nowhere, Mark had paused, his hand behind Maggie's ear, and said, so seriously she could've died, "Do you steal things often? Is this something we need to talk about?"

She'd nuzzled her mouth against his neck. She was mortified and yet, at the same time, found she was also overcome with lust, with love, with an exact and perfect balance of the two. "Never," she said. "Never." They'd fallen asleep on the covers that night, both condoms in the travel-pack successfully and happily put to use.

Maggie turned in her seat and watched the last of the turbines disappear from view.

"All gone," said Mark. "Only five hundred seventy-seven miles to go."

Somehow it was already three o'clock.

4

After the Indianapolis beltway, they stopped at the first gas station with green space. Mark had done as instructed and tuned in to the AM weather station. His father was right: there were alerts and advisories and warnings for everything east of Cincinnati. Blackouts had started. Towns off 64 were already being declared disaster zones. The storms had originated in the east and now were headed west. They were headed directly toward Mark and Maggie — that's how she'd put it anyway, Mark wouldn't be so histrionic — which meant US-35 would probably be black, too, by the time they crossed into Ohio.

Maggie proposed checking her computer, just to see the full extent of what they were getting themselves into. But Mark balked. They'd had a good stretch, the two of them. Where they were, the sun was still shining. Gerome had been quiet, Maggie had been sweet, and Mark had lucked into a miraculously uninterrupted set of the Stones and Petty. But then, pulling into the station, gassing up, Maggie had to go and suggest getting out the computer and researching the storm, as if what her phone could access wasn't already enough. "There are probably pictures," she'd said. "We could see what the devastation looks like." It was her use of that word—*devastation*—that had immediately soured his mood. She sounded like one of those news anchors, delirious with the possibility of tragedy.

The thing was, the suggestion itself to get out the computer wasn't half bad. They could have used it to look for hotels. If the situation was as dire as the broadcasts were saying, then it might have been nice to have a sure thing waiting for them when the storm came. But the quiver in Maggie's voice had riled him with its intimation that their lives—*their* lives: Maggie's and his—were somehow suddenly at risk. She'd gone and gotten desperate, illogical—"This could be bad. This could be Katrina bad. Sandy bad"—which had killed his driving buzz completely.

Nope. He wasn't about to give in to the computer. He'd so far resisted bringing it into his classroom (to the ire of his colleagues), and he would resist, for as long as possible, bringing it into every aspect of their lives.

A few years back, Mark's father turned him on to some intriguing articles about server farms and data barns, articles suggesting that the move from paper to e-readers wasn't nearly as green or eco-friendly as his and most other universities were insisting. Plus, the Internet's energy consumption was something like ten billion watts of electricity in the United States alone, with another twenty billion in the rest of the world, which was equivalent to the output of something like thirty nuclear power plants, which—come on!—was a wholly mind-boggling statistic. Once a month or so, whenever Robert forwarded a new series of articles, Mark printed one or two of them out, made a couple dozen copies off campus (no way was he going to use his copy card and risk a lecture from the chair), and then posted them in the department hallways.

The point? Fuck the computer. How had they secured hotels

in the past on road trips? The old-fashioned way: by stopping and asking if there was a room.

"They probably don't even have Wi-Fi here," Mark said.

"They have Wi-Fi everywhere," she said.

"How about this? After dinner we'll find a hotel, and then you can knock yourself out all you want on that thing."

She hadn't responded, but he could tell her brain had returned to whatever haunted house it had been popping in on since news of the college girl. He hated to resent a dead woman, one who'd died so ignominiously, but he'd nearly gotten Maggie back. She'd almost been restored to him. Instead, he could see from her face — the trembling lower lip she was biting to keep calm — that she was already playing out worst-case scenarios: a tree in the road, which would lead to a blocked avenue, which would lead to an unfamiliar route, which would lead to a dead end, which would lead to the Bates Motel. It was too much.

"I'll get the coffee," he said.

Five minutes later, he was standing inside the gas station's coffee shop/convenience mart, and he was watching Maggie walk Gerome. The two of them were going back and forth over a narrow strip of grass. Gerome wasn't doing anything but sniffing. Maggie was talking to him — he could see from inside, see her lips moving — probably trying to coax him into lifting his leg. But Gerome was ignoring her. If he didn't want to pee, he wasn't going to. No amount of baby talk was going to change that.

Who was that woman out there? And what was the possibility that he'd actually spend his life with her? His whole life? Think about it: what were the actual odds? There were statistics on these sorts of things. If he wanted, he could probably walk down the hall to Sociology and get the exact and most-up-to-date numbers on his chances of staying married. Mark's guess? The odds were against them. The odds probably said that they had another four, maybe five years together. Which was about how many years Gerome had left. But then, if that were the case, if that's how he really felt, then why'd he marry her at all? And hadn't they survived the first seven — okay, maybe not this most recent one, but the six before that and the three before marriage — hadn't they survived those years in style, with class? She hadn't cheated. Neither had he. He'd never even thought about it.

Okay, sure, fine, yes. There was Elizabeth, his former research assistant. But they hadn't touched. Not once! Plus, she'd dropped out of the program last spring. Academia, she told him, wasn't for her. And over the summer she'd moved to California, so it's not as though they could have messed around even if they wanted to. But, fine — all things on the table? — there had been some e-mails, and those didn't look good for anyone.

In the past, he'd made a point of checking his work correspondence only once a week. He even had a little caveat about it on his syllabus: *Contrary to popular belief, professors do not, in fact, sit at their computers all day long waiting for the next student missive. If you e-mail me, it should be important. If you e-mail me, you should expect to wait at least one week before hearing back.* Every Friday he went to campus specifically to check e-mail and catch up on student communication. It usually took four or five hours to sort through and respond, but he preferred losing one large block of time once a week to losing minnow-bite moments here and there every day. Imagine how quickly a day — a life! — could be subsumed by those moments if you let it. The thought made him itch.

But then, last fall, he'd gotten that first e-mail from Elizabeth: "If I called you devilishly handsome, would you mind? And if I told you that I think about you, what then?"

It was Elizabeth who'd first brought his attention to the group of online activists who called themselves Anonymous. She'd suggested it as the final chapter for his book, not that he was anywhere close to being finished. But the chapters were outlined, and Elizabeth, he suspected rightly, had said his history would be incomplete if it failed to address the *future* of anonymity. He'd been too myopic in his research, focusing almost entirely on pretenses that led to death — stonings, masked hangmen, firing squads, kill buttons on death row. He'd been looking down and back instead of up and out. It meant so much more research. It meant creating a new timeline and giving into a delayed deadline. It meant delving into a world of materials that existed entirely online. The irony didn't elude him; his colleagues would chide him — "The luddite takes on the Internet," they'd say when they caught wind — but Elizabeth was right. It wasn't just Anonymous. It was Occupy. It was crowdsourcing. There was anonymity in inclusiveness, a "we" instead of an "I" that meant an end to ownership and the possibility of meaningful blame. *Anyone* was starting to feel very much like *everyone*. But Mark wasn't there yet; wasn't yet ready to draw the necessary conclusions or complete the larger argument. It was a process, one step at a time. The chapters needed to build on one another, and Elizabeth had taught him the importance of surprise, of the willingness to be surprised by what he found. It was essential that, while he might have a theory — a working theory — it not be set in stone until he was absolutely ready. She'd opened up a whole new approach. He'd have called her his muse if it wouldn't have sounded so outrageous.

Before writing her back, he'd switched over from his professional account to his personal one. He avoided answering either of her questions directly, instead asking her about life after academia.

That was nearly nine months ago, just after the mugging. Now he checked his e-mail daily, whenever he was on campus and sometimes when he walked Gerome alone. He changed the passwords on both accounts so that it was no longer Maggie's birthday: sign number one that he knew his back-and-forth with Elizabeth wasn't on the up-and-up. Sign number two was that he sometimes thought of her, alone, in the shower, and one time during sex with Maggie. She, Elizabeth, came from a grossly conservative family in New England, and she was grossly conservative herself. But she made Mark laugh and she had this *joie de vivre*, this confidence that, perhaps because he knew it came from money, made him want to snatch her up and bend her over. But it was sign number three that really mattered, sign number three that told him in no uncertain terms that he was definitely crossing a line: if he'd caught wind of Maggie doing anything remotely similar: texting, e-mailing, straight-up flirting the way he'd been doing — he'd be furious.

He took another look at Maggie, at her long limbs and good posture — *That's my wife, goddamn it! Wife!* — no, not furious: he'd be livid. And there it was.

5

It was a childish habit — checking under all the doors in a public washroom to make sure someone wasn't lurking — because what would Maggie do if she actually found someone? Scream? Fight back? Wilt? Yet she could never resist the urge.

In this particular bathroom, Maggie discovered only one pair of feet. They were at the far end of the glinty silver latrine, behind the final stall door, which was closed and, presumably, locked. And they were turned, these feet were, in the wrong direction — as if the person attached to them might be barfing or about to flush the toilet. Maggie hurried back to the opposite end of the room, taking the toilet closest to the exit. She locked the door, covered the seat with paper, squatted so her skin wasn't even touching, then started peeing as quickly as possible.

She was acutely aware of the sound coming from the only other compartment in use. Or, rather, she was aware of a lack of sound. Though she loathed in general the prospect of listening to another person pee (or worse), she was further loath to find herself in an enclosed space with someone who wasn't using it for its intended purpose. She knew about public restrooms. Everybody knew about public restrooms. At the girls' school she'd attended when she was little, a teacher had been raped in one of the stalls after hours. It was her first encounter with the word. She'd taken it home to her mother, without yet comprehending its meaning. From the way her teacher had said it, she'd understood that the word had negative connotations. But when her mother explained it, jabbing her index finger into the invisible air between them, Maggie thought she might faint from embarrassment. "Never mind," she'd said, backing up slowly. "Never mind," she'd said again, as though she could undo her sudden new knowledge; undo the existence of the word's meaning altogether.

Still squatting, Maggie bent over even farther and angled herself so that she could peek — her shorts around her knees — under the partition in the direction of the far toilet. Though there were several stalls between them, she could clearly make out the feet, which were now firmly facing in Maggie's direction. She sat up clumsily; the tiniest splash of urine landed on her underwear.

She closed her eyes and flushed; her heart practiced handspeed drills against her breastplate. An image — one that didn't belong to her, one that belonged, if at all, to the coed — skimmed along the backs of her eyelids, a pebble across a pond. The detectives had worked up to the more gruesome photographs. They'd started with a shot of the coed's building. Then a shot of the coed herself — professionally taken, nondescript gray background, cocked head, sweet but canned smile. The third photo was of the back of her head. An oval bruise was below the hairline, just above the nape of her neck. Her chin — what Maggie could see of her chin from the angle of the camera — was pushed up against the base of a toilet. Maggie had looked up at the detectives. "It's just like my bruise," she'd said, massaging her neck. They'd nodded. They'd felt so certain — the three of them — that it must have been the same man. But by the time they'd run the gamut of mug shots — there'd been a witness to the murder — they discovered it wasn't. Mark, when he got home, after he saw the cops standing over her and then had seen what they'd been showing her, was furious. "What I'm trying to figure out," he kept saying, pacing toward the kitchen table, then away from it, "is why you felt the need to show her these?" He'd grabbed at the photos of the coed, but they'd swiped them from his reach. "Explain the logic," he kept saying. "Just help me understand." It was Maggie who showed the detectives to the door. And in the morning, it was Maggie — though she knew it wasn't the same man; they all did — who began surfing the web for pocket pistols. Online, she discovered a whole world dedicated entirely to personal defense. She'd found it utterly entrancing.

She used an elbow now to push her way hastily out of the stall, nearly racing to the bathroom's exit.

Outside the sun was blinding, the air thick. She took a deep breath, then exhaled steadily.

It was hard to believe they were headed in the direction of a multi-state storm, but she'd gotten out her phone while she was walking Gerome and a brief search had turned up some legitimately brutal photos as evidence — loose power lines, homes with trees resting on their roofs. An old man was dead, though that might have been an unrelated story. Still.

Gerome hadn't peed when she walked him, but at least he'd gotten to stretch his legs.

She made a beeline across the parking lot in the direction of the car. She'd left the windows cracked, but Maggie knew it sometimes took fewer than fifteen minutes for a dog to die from heat stroke. She'd seen it too many times before.

A man dressed as a cowboy tipped his hat in her direction as they crossed paths on the asphalt.

"Nice tits," he said.

She stopped, then turned. Instinctively, she raised a hand to her chest, a protective gesture. A man was accosting her in broad daylight. She couldn't believe it.

"Excuse me?" she said.

The man, who had also stopped and turned, also said, "Excuse me?"

"What did you say to me?" Her therapist had once told her that, for victims, confrontation could be a powerful tool. To ignore new moments of vulnerability might be to encourage preexisting fear.

"Ma'am?"

"Just now," said Maggie, "what did you say?"

"Did I say something?"

"You did."

Except now Maggie wasn't sure. Now she was confused. She'd heard the word so precisely: *tits.* But now the voice she perceived in her head didn't match up with the one this cowboy was using. Evidence indicated that babies, after birth, could distinguish sounds once heard in utero. Maggie wondered now if she'd plucked this word — this *tits* — from a memory, from a memory of a memory, or, worse, from an article she'd read earlier that morning. Space, as a concept, kept a certain type of person awake at night — its vastness; its ceaselessness; the notion, for instance, that the Milky Way itself was a blip on something numinously more massive. What sometimes kept Maggie awake was the idea of auditory dimensions and the infinitesimally imperceptible regions of her own head. It was possible she'd been hallucinating, but possible also that her energetic id had an internal voice that had chosen this moment to introduce itself.

"Did I wish you a nice day?" the man said. "My wife says I'm always wishing people nice days. She says I'm on autopilot half the time. Half the time, she says, I have no idea what I'm saying."

A woman in the distance whistled.

The cowboy turned, gave a thumbs-up, then looked back at Maggie. "There she is now. Bet you anything I'm in hot water just for talking to you." He tipped his hat again. "Nice day," he said. Then he was gone.

Maggie didn't know what to say, only what not to say. She would *not* be telling Mark about this. He wouldn't have believed her.

Immediately beneath Maggie's moccasins was a freshly paved twelve-inch surface covering made of sand and rock glued together with man-made hydrocarbons, beneath which was a six-inch layer of recycled asphalt product, beneath which was an underlayment of gravel, beneath which — deep, deep, deep beneath — was the continental crust itself, igneous, metamorphic, sedimentary. Some twenty miles beneath the crust was the lithosphere, beneath which was the asthenosphere, beneath which was the upper mantel, beneath which was the liquid outer core, beneath which was the solid inner core, where — on this particular day — the temperature was just shy of 10,800°F, as hot as the surface of the sun.

Some thirty-nine thousand miles above, Maggie shivered.

6

The barista called his name. Mark turned to pick up the order only to find a large man in a Western-style hat standing between him and the counter. The man was gazing out the massive tinted window of the gas station in the direction of Maggie, who was now cleaning off the windshield with one of those convenience wipers they leave between pumps.

"You know the one about how to tell a wife from a girlfriend?" It was the man talking, though he wasn't looking at Mark. He was still looking out the window.

"Pardon me?" said Mark.

"It's a joke," the man said. "The joke is that a girlfriend looks like she's just had a good fucking and —"

Mark coughed. "You have me confused with someone who's interested." He stepped in front of the man and picked up the coffees.

The man stepped with him, resting an elbow on the counter so that Mark's immediate path to the exit was blocked.

"A wife," the man said, nodding his hat in the direction of the window, "looks like she needs one."

"You just said what to me?" Mark thought maybe the barista would intervene, but he was at the cash register at the other end of the counter, taking someone else's order.

"I'm fucking with you, Bucko." The man laughed. "Just two guys joshing around. I like your wife. It's a compliment."

This was the problem with gas stations, with rest stops in general. They were teeming with chance encounters between human beings who, under any other circumstance, would have no reason or opportunity to engage.

The question now was how to respond. Was there an action Mark could take that would be nobler than another? He wasn't sure, in this case, if Maggie needed defending. She wasn't present and hadn't heard and therefore couldn't be personally wounded. And yet to say nothing seemed potentially cowardly. He felt unsure of his role, his duty. Perhaps it was best in these instances — always best — simply to move on and away as quickly as possible, which was what he did, shoving past the man, a cup in either hand.

"Screw off," Mark said.

Behind him, over the sound of the bell above the exit, which jingled now as he pushed his way out the door, he thought he heard the man laughing. He didn't turn around to check.

When Mark got back to the car, Gerome was in the backseat panting and Maggie was already in the driver's seat. She'd recapped the gas tank and returned the hose to the filling station. Now she was monkeying with the center vents, adjusting the air stream so that it was aimed squarely at the dog's face.

Mark put the coffees on the hood of the car and opened the door.

"What's wrong?" Maggie said.

He handed in the first coffee, and she put it in the cup holder.

"You look like you've seen a ghost," she said.

Mark was sometimes startled by the way Maggie could read his face so quickly and effectively. It gave him the feeling that she was always aware of him, always aware of exactly where he was and what he was doing — whether she could see him or not.

He handed her the second coffee. "Nothing," he said, "just ready to get where we're going."

"Pit stops," she said. "No one's favorite part of a road trip." She secured the second cup firmly in its place. "Would-be cowboys are the worst."

Mark followed Maggie's gaze. In the distance, next to a large pickup truck with an after-market pair of plastic testicles hanging from the bumper, a man was looking their way.

Together they watched as he placed a large-brimmed hat on his head and tipped it in their direction.

"What made you say that?" Mark asked.

"Say what?"

"About cowboys."

Maggie chewed at her lower lip. She was deciding whether or not to say something. Abruptly, she shrugged. "No reason," she said. She buckled her seat belt, then glanced up at the rearview mirror and adjusted it slightly. "Just that people don't seem to mind their business like they used to. You know?"

Out the window, just to the right of Maggie's profile, a minivan trying to exit the station honked at a sedan taking too long to turn. There was a second honk, then a third, then an extended uninterrupted fourth that received stares from all around.

Mark scanned the parking lot. The truck and its driver were gone. "I know," he said. He reached over and knocked on the steering wheel. "Let's blow this joint."

They pulled out into traffic. It was four-thirty. The sun was a magnificent orange.

Mark felt bad for not telling Maggie the truth about the

stranger in the gas station and the crude joke that had been made at her expense. But, he reasoned, in many ways he was protecting her. He was sheltering her from the quiet horror that actually *did* exist in their world. This wasn't the stuff of her news articles or crime procedurals. This was worse because it was real, because it potentially affected *them*.

Be more patient, he told himself. *Be more patient*.

7

They crossed into Ohio just after five. It was light out still, but the nature of the sky had changed. The ceilings were lower than when they'd passed the turbines in Indiana. The trees along the highway pushed back against an unseen current, and the leaves showed green, then silver, then green again. The car's windows whistled like teakettles — high, plaintive, stiff. A few times Maggie drifted into the rumble strip because the wind was so strong. Gerome had whined each time, but Mark didn't say a thing. He'd been silent since their pit stop.

Out of nowhere, the GPS system — which they used primarily to count down the miles, since they knew the drive inside and out, backwards and forwards — started beeping. Maggie had just taken exit 1 off I-70 in the direction of Eaton. Gerome shifted behind them but didn't get up.

"It's mad at me," Maggie said, tapping the monitor. She said this more to hear a voice — any voice — than to be heard by her husband.

Mark punched a few buttons. "It wants us to stay on 70 until 75," he said. "Then go through Dayton."

"We never go through Dayton." She watched the screen images change while Mark continued to push buttons. "What did that mean? That last message?"

Mark didn't answer, just turned the system off altogether. "We can keep track of the miles on the odometer," he said.

"But what did that mean?" said Maggie.

"What?"

"*Restricted usage road* — what did that mean?"

"It didn't say that."

"It did," said Maggie. "Turn it back on."

Her neck went hot. Mark was staring. She could feel his attention, though she refused to look his way. He'd caught the tenor of her voice, its unsteadiness. But if he thought she was imagining something awful, he was wrong. This time he was wrong. She simply didn't see why they couldn't consult the GPS every now and then. Wasn't that why they had it? For instance, what if there was a required detour or a road that was freshly out of service? All she hoped to do was save them time, avoid preventable trouble.

On the Enneagram, there was a pair of statements that perfectly summed up the current situation, as well as their opposing takes: *I've been careful and have tried to prepare for unforeseen problems* (Maggie). *I've been spontaneous and have preferred to improvise as problems come up* (Mark). Or so Maggie imagined; Mark had never taken the test.

Fine, then. Forget the GPS. Hope, after all, was the confusion of desire with probability, or however the saying went. But if they ended up having to "improvise" by taking a detour or turning around, getting back on 70 and going through Dayton — well, if they ended up having to do that, she'd have a hard time not gloating. That's for sure.

"*Restricted road usage,*" said Mark, "is a ploy to keep away through traffic from smaller towns. It's just a way to funnel us to a toll."

He was probably right, but she'd never seen such a notice before when they'd made the drive, and she knew he hadn't either. No matter. Just then, she didn't feel compelled to engage. She'd learned that winning was often about who could be quiet longest. This wasn't a theory she had discussed with her therapist — in part because she suspected it might have been deemed morbid, perhaps even destructive — but in silence was power. In Maggie's ability to ignore her husband was the added bonus of occasionally making him feel as though he'd been dismissed or, better, as though he'd been the one to overreact, not her. And so she focused on the road — on its double yellow lines, its faint bend to the east — and said nothing.

After a little while, Mark turned away from her. Maggie cracked the front window and the car howled. This got Gerome's attention. He stood, stretched, then sniffed at the air, at all the midwestern smells filtering in. Chickens. Hay. Cows. Manure.

They were on US-35, headed southeast into Ohio. The sun was slanted low and bright to their right, in spite of the copper clouds ahead of them. The air itself was tea-toned, a pinkish brown, almost shiny. The angle of the light seemed funny, somehow off, as though the sun were being reflected back and forth by the darkening storm clouds and its position wasn't exactly what it should have been. A magic trick. A sleight of hand. Prestidigitation in the sky.

This — US-35 — was the ugliest leg of their trip, and they'd be on it for the next couple hundred miles or so, until it dumped them into West Virginia and onto Interstate 64. Maggie almost always drove this stretch. She didn't mind the reduced speeds, and she wasn't too bothered by all the stoplights. They were punctuations in an otherwise uneventful trip. Don't misunderstand: she didn't actively enjoy these 200-some miles—who could? —but she didn't ... Well, she didn't take their ugliness personally, the way Mark sometimes seemed to.

To her, Ohio was just sad. Sad and neglected. A state that didn't know it was already dead. Like animals at a kill shelter. They didn't know that all that water and all that food didn't mean anything about the possibility of a future. All it meant was that some good people were fighting a war they'd already lost. What the animals couldn't know: they were already dead.

As a pre-vet, she'd been acutely aware of the rancor non-pre-vets felt for kill shelters. But Maggie and her peers never chimed in when the outsiders started up. They understood, and Maggie in particular—without any of them then having all the facts—that kill shelters existed in the same way no-kill shelters did. Nobody *wanted* to kill the animals—nobody who volunteered at a shelter, anyway: she'd read the article last week about those kids up in New York who poured lighter fluid on a three-legged dog and then set it on fire. But that was different. With kill shelters, the reasoning was straightforward: the money and space simply didn't exist to maintain the animals while they might have waited to be adopted. The idea that volunteers at kill shelters were happy about all those soon-to-die kittens and puppies? A preposterous notion, which brought her back to Ohio: just because you were born there, just because you had been raised there and hadn't had the sense or opportunity to get out, that didn't mean it was your fault. In the game of geography, you and yours simply hadn't lucked out.

Mark, though—and Maggie knew the diatribe by heart because she'd heard it dozens of times before—he believed that Ohio deserved itself. Those first few times during the early years of their marriage when they'd made the mistake of stopping at major travel plazas and witnessing firsthand the overweight families in their over-large T-shirts eating their oversized meals in their over-tall cars — the sight had filled Mark, every time, with a noiseless sort of rage that could last all the way to Virginia, to his parents' farm. And Maggie knew this for a fact because she'd felt the noiselessness in those early years; she'd been the recipient of its meanness. She, not Ohio, was the one who handled that odium, and so, very quickly, she established a new route — one that favored the smaller, slower roads they were taking now — and she volunteered to drive the segment so that Mark might sleep his way through.

Ahead, in the far, far distance, there was a crack of lightning.

"Did you see that?" said Mark.

Maggie rolled up the window. They car sealed itself with a *whump*. A sign on the side of the road indicated that the speed limit would reduce in the next mile.

Mark messed with the radio. "We should try to get Gerome to do something sometime soon," he said. He stopped at a weather station. Local schools were already being canceled on Monday. It was only Saturday.

Maggie nodded. "I agree," she said. "You were right. We'll need a hotel."

"I should have let you find us one online," he said. "You'd have gotten us a deal."

"A smoking deal," she said. It was a phrase Mark's parents used indiscriminately, on anything from a Parisian hotel room to a bundle of asparagus purchased at the local farmer's market.

Maggie put a hand on Mark's knee, and he, without a moment's hesitation, reached down and squeezed her fingers.

See? That was just the thing. The thing that kept them together. He understood her. He, too, recognized that though they might approach their opinions — say, of Ohio or even the GPS for that matter — from different directions, ultimately those directions landed them in the same place, with the same result. Each knew that the other was theirs. Two brains thinking one thought. Two brains following one final wave of logic. She felt a nearly animalistic sense of intimacy at that moment.

It was true, regrettably so, that in the last few weeks Maggie's brain had been going out of its way to seek out extra tangents, to explore other prospects — darker, more disturbing possibilities — but that was her *brain*. That wasn't her. And her brain was beyond her control. *You can do what you will, but you can't will what you will*, another aphorism she'd been taught by her therapist.

But therapists and aphorisms aside, the takeaway was this: Mark was hers and she was his, and everything, ultimately, in one way or another, would always work out between them.

The radio went silent. There was another crack of lightning in the distance. Then there was static. Then, with no formality or warning, the radio issued several long low beeps. A tornado watch was underway in southeast Ohio.

In 1840 the Great Natchez tornado killed 317 people in Natchez, Mississippi. In 1925 the Tri-State tornado ran a path of 219 miles for nearly four hours, from Missouri to Illinois to Indiana. More than 600 people died. In 1989 roughly 1,300 people were killed by the Daulatpur-Saturia tornado in Bangladesh. Twelve thousand people were injured. Eighty thousand were left homeless.

The tornado — that funnel-shaped weapon capable of moving at nearly 70 miles an hour with internal rotational winds of sometimes 250 — is no laughing matter.

8

Maggie pulled the car into a small Shell station. They were somewhere in New Lebanon — population 4,000 — a place where US-35 felt more like a side street than a highway. Squat ranchers, secondhand shops, the occasional empty bank.

Next to the station, thankfully, there was an overgrown field of grass. Maggie had only just turned on the windshield wipers. The rain wasn't too bad yet.

"I'll walk him," said Mark. "Unless you want to and then I'll top up the tank instead."

"Your choice," she said.

Gerome was standing with his front paws on the center console. He was whining, asking a question — *whu, whu, whu* — whose end he couldn't achieve. Gerome hated to get rained on probably as much if not more than Mark. They had that in common. *Smart boy,* thought Mark.

"Smart boy," said Mark, massaging the dog's chin. "You think this is shit, too, eh?" He turned in his seat, dug around in the floorboard behind him, and found Gerome's leash. The dog continued his plea.

To Maggie, he said, "I'll do it." Mark's knees were cramping; a short walk would do him good.

Maggie got out and started the pump. After a second, she ducked her head back inside the car where Mark was still fidgeting with the leash. "You want anything? The card reader's not working. I have to go in to pay."

"Coffee?" Mark said. "If it's hot?"

"You got it." She trotted off across the parking lot toward the store, the wind pushing her ponytail, her shirt, the hem of her shorts to the side. It seemed her clothes, the pieces of her, were aligned with the earth and not Maggie.

Mark pulled down his baseball cap and coaxed Gerome from the backseat.

"Come on, guy," Mark said. "We're in this together."

Gerome put his tail between his legs and emitted a bleat of objection, but he hopped down from the car without a struggle.

The little field to the side of the station was already soggy. Mark walked Gerome the length of it so that he, Mark, could stay on the concrete and Gerome could walk on the grass. But Gerome wasn't having it. Instead, he balanced his paws along the concrete perimeter, looking up at Mark every now and then as if to say, "If you don't have to, I don't have to."

Meanwhile Maggie was taking her time in the store. The parking lot was empty except for a beat-up pickup, which probably belonged to whatever sad sack was working inside. There couldn't have been other customers. Mark imagined Maggie in the women's restroom, pulling little pieces of toilet paper from the roll and arranging them daintily around the seat. Then, out of nowhere, he thought of Elizabeth, her severe short hair, her lithe little body. She'd played volleyball as an undergrad at some small liberal arts school in the Northeast, something she'd mentioned as a throwaway as they outlined his upcoming chapters. She hadn't yet told him she was dropping out of the program. "It's not merely about the body," she'd said. "It's about discipline. It's about pushing the brain." She spoke with authority about everything, with an air of privilege and a sense of too much self-importance. He'd liked it. Her entitlement was a bulletproof jacket, and she'd clearly been making her way through life as if nothing would ever thwart her.

Now he imagined Elizabeth in the stall next to Maggie. He gave her a skirt, which was hiked unceremoniously to her waist, and panties pushed just to the knee. Above the toilet, she maintained a perfect athletic squat, never once letting the skin of her thighs touch the porcelain.

Mark's glutes flexed instinctively. There was a tingling in his hamstrings from his knees to his pelvis. Gerome pulled at the leash. That afternoon when Elizabeth had told him about volleyball was more than a year ago. Now she was elsewhere, in some West Coast town probably dating some West Coast asshole. In their correspondence, Mark never wrote explicitly about desire, and normally she didn't either. But in an e-mail she'd sent just that week — in fact, on the very day Mark had discovered the switchblade and then decided without discussion that they would leave Chicago ahead of schedule — Elizabeth had broached the subject point-blank.

Hiya—
So I've been thinking about sex.

Mark had gotten up from his chair and closed his office door before continuing. The muscles in his buttocks tightened as he sat back down, and he was reminded of a day from childhood when Gwen had explained why horses so often relieved themselves before fleeing. "They're lightening their load," she'd told him. His father had said, "In other words, they've had the crap scared out of them."

Hiya—

So I've been thinking about sex. And I've been thinking about your book. It would be incomplete, you know, if you didn't also address what's happening in the world of sex vis-à-vis anonymity. Like, did you know there's a whole section on Craigslist about conference meet-ups? You name it; they have it. Think about it: the world's most intimate act becomes anonymous by way of the Internet. Brilliant! These are real-life hookups, real-life liaisons. But when they're over, they're over, and nobody knows anyone else's name. Husbands, wives, the people back home—they never find out. You just get on a plane and get out of Dodge. So my question is this—

The e-mail had gone on, but he couldn't think about that right now. Gerome still hadn't peed and the rain was picking up, and Mark was determined not to get back in the car until the dog had done something. He didn't want a repeat of the morning. The two times Gerome squatted—he almost never lifted his leg—a car drove by and the rainwater splashing up under its tires distracted him.

Mark could feel himself getting rankled. He knew being mad at a dog was irrational. You can't reason with an animal. But he couldn't help it. He was peeved. "Come on, man," he said. "Come on."

Finally, just as Maggie emerged from the little store, Gerome squatted and peed.

"You took forever," Mark called from across the parking lot. His shoulders were wet from the rain, the tops of his shoes damp.

Maggie shrugged. She had a coffee in each hand and a little

plastic bag hooked around her wrist. "Yeah, but Gerome's just now doing his business," she said. "So what does it matter?"

The coffee, like Mark knew it would be, was lukewarm.

"This is bad," he said.

"I'll drink it," Maggie said.

But that wasn't the point. Mark wanted coffee. He needed the caffeine.

Maggie pulled the car back onto 35. Gerome was standing in the backseat. He was drooling — something he did when he was nervous. It drove Mark nuts that they had a neurotic dog. Neurotic people had neurotic dogs, and Mark was not a neurotic person. And Maggie was a vet, for Christ's sake. It made no sense that Gerome wasn't a more natural animal.

"I swear to god, your dog is going to kill me if he doesn't sit down," Mark said.

Maggie was ignoring him. Or, rather, she was ignoring his pessimism. Or what she'd call his pessimism. Which was an imprecise term for his current state of mind. What she *meant* by pessimism — even though she hadn't said anything, but what she meant in her thoughts, which right now Mark could've read a mile away — was, in fact, his current *dissatisfaction*. That's what she was actually ignoring. She didn't like it when he complained about more than one thing at a time: the coffee, the dog.

Well, tough luck. Sometimes the cookie crumbled in an unforgiving way, and sometimes Mark just needed to spout off about it. Sometimes it felt dishonest to keep his grievances to himself, which was what Maggie would have preferred.

He took another sip of coffee and grimaced deliberately, even though he knew Maggie was looking at the road and not at him. It felt good to grimace. It felt good to indulge in a physical manifestation of his dissatisfaction. He grimaced again. He felt like a man. *A man's man*, he thought. *A dog's dog and a man's man.* But

Gerome was not a dog's dog. Where had that thought even come from? He shook it off.

Maggie switched the wipers to a higher speed. Outside, the air was glossy. Cotton ball clouds gathered overhead — milk blue at the bottom but rich green high up where the red sun hit the rounding peaks. In the distance, above a blinking streetlight, there were multiple cracks of sepia lightning.

"They were running on a generator," Maggie said after a moment. "The gas station."

"A generator?" said Mark. "I guess you don't need power to pump gas, huh? Or maybe you do. I hadn't thought about it."

"The guy said all the houses on his side of the street lost power. All the houses on the other side" — she pointed out Mark's window — "still have it."

For a moment, he watched the houses, one after the other. Some with cars in the driveway, most empty. Some with tidily mown lawns, most not. In almost every yard, there was a child's abandoned toy — a car, a castle, a shovel. If they'd had a kid, Mark would have avoided the brightly colored plastics, the neon yellows and greens that were geared more toward safety than fun. Not just for ecological reasons would he eschew the plastics, but for sentimental ones. Like so many others of his generation, he'd grown up with a classic red metal wagon: first he'd been carted around in it by his parents, and then, later, when he was big enough to pull it himself, he'd used it to tow the pots and pans and wooden spatulas Gwen had given him as playthings. He used his imagination to color in the fantasies, to brighten those hours of magical aloneness he spent outdoors. If they'd ever had a child, Mark would have raised him the same way. But, of course, they didn't. There was no one to be raised in or out of his image, which was simply the fact of the matter.

"In ten more years, towns like this won't exist," Mark said. "Did you see all those For Sale signs? Everything is empty. It's just not cost-effective to live in the middle of nowhere. It's irresponsible."

"Your parents live in the middle of nowhere," she said.

"It's different. They live off the grid."

"No," she said. "They don't. They aren't farmers. They're retirees. They couldn't live without access to the city."

"My father still teaches."

"He's emeritus. He teaches once a year," she said. Then, after a beat: "When he feels like it."

Mark didn't understand why she was being so aggressive, perhaps because he'd been finicky about the coffee. "You love my parents," he said.

"I do love your parents," she said. "I love them more than my own. I don't know what I'd do without them in my life."

Other wives made similar avowals to their husbands and they didn't mean a single word. But something Mark loved about Maggie — something he was genuinely thankful for — was that she did love his parents. And they loved her. They'd taken her in so keenly, so dearly. Maggie had a way of bringing out the best in Robert and Gwen. Around her, their eccentricities fell away. His mother especially seemed to understand, without ever being explicitly told, that Maggie's childhood had been — to put it kindly — subpar. Maggie was the first girl with whom his mother hadn't tried to compete. Instead, Gwen — like Mark, like Robert — had fallen quite quickly in love with Maggie.

"I only meant," he said, "that if they wanted, they could live without access to the city. But they don't want to."

Maggie nodded. "I know," she said. "I'm sorry. I know exactly what you meant. I'm being snippy. My mind is somewhere else."

Mark had a great affinity for Maggie's mind. He'd fallen first, yes, for her looks — that goofy gap between her teeth hidden always just behind her plump upper lip. But he'd been seduced ultimately by her brain — its quirks, its ambitions. There were nights still when he would wake with a start, fearing the evening on the riverboat had been a dream, fearing he'd never met her. Lately, though, he was frightened that her mind might be morphing. He wanted desperately to keep it safe and steady.

"Where is it now?" he said. "Your mind? What are you thinking?"

"Are you making fun?"

"Not at all," he said. "Tell me."

She massaged the steering wheel with both hands. After a minute, she said, "Do you think you willfully see the worst in people?"

"How do you mean? I don't understand."

"Typically speaking, do you think you've been pessimistic or optimistic?"

"Optimistic," he said. "Where's this coming from?"

"Typically speaking," she said, "do you think you've been even-tempered or are you prone to moodiness?"

"Moodiness?" he said. "Is this part of your test?"

"Strong changes of mood," she said. "Like with the coffee."

"I suppose ..." he said. He searched for a real answer. He didn't want her to retreat, but he also didn't want to be tricked into taking some adulterated version of a test he had no faith in and whose results — accurate or otherwise — proved nothing. "I suppose you were feeling snippy just now and I was feeling moody. I think we can safely blame the weather and the drive for both."

Maggie was right — what she was suggesting but hadn't come directly out and said — Mark did find occasional pleasure in predicting life's disappointments, but she was wrong to suspect him of seeing the worst in people. He saw the best. He did! It was why he taught, why he was a teacher in the first place. He believed in humanity, in the generosity of the human spirit, in the individual: *My heart leaps up!* It was the Internet that had gotten in the way, eliminating face-to-face interaction, obviating the need, the desire, the occasion to see the whites of another's eyes. Strip it from them and they'd all go back to normal. It, normalcy, was still attainable. Real childhood could still be salvaged: *The Child is father of the Man!* Maybe not for the ones who had already been exposed, but they could be treated. Like for a virus. They could be weaned slowly off it. The Internet was a teat, a drug. Take it away — cut those thirty billion watts of electricity — and they'd get used to it. They'd become human again: *Bound each to each by natural piety.* He was sure of it. Elizabeth had once called him a breathtaking teacher.

To their right, they were now passing a single-story structure with a sign overhead: PINEY CAMP HOTEL. There was grass growing up its sides, but there were a few cars parked in front. He thought again of Elizabeth. She could have made a place like Piney Camp fun; would have called it an adventure, maybe even a breathtaking one. *So I've been thinking about sex,* she'd written. Without too much effort, he could picture the kind of life they might have had together if he'd been younger, single, if she'd really been an option: road trips for the sake of it to towns they'd never heard of. He could practically hear her saying, "It has a bed, doesn't it? Is there anything more we need?"

Mark squeezed his temples. He needed to snap out of it.

Part of it — You know what? Yes, though he'd never thought of it this way before: part of what made Maggie's intense new relationship with fear so intolerable was that it felt like a comment about him. That switchblade, those cans of mace, that outrageous application for a concealed carry permit — it all felt like maybe Maggie didn't think he could protect her if and when she needed protection. Sure, he'd not been with her in the alley, but if he had been, he could have done something. He could have pushed the guy down or stepped in front of her and told her to run. He could have done any number of things. It wasn't his fault he wasn't there. Just like it wasn't his fault that the college girl was dead. It was coincidence they lived near her at all; coincidence that both women at the hands of different men had been hit in the neck with the heel of a gun. But there was something about Maggie's newfound paranoia, about her determination that she was suddenly more susceptible to another attack than someone else, that made Mark feel like less of a man.

Yes: less of a man. That right there was the problem. It was devastating.

9

The rain picked up. The sky turned dark and slick. If there was a moon, they couldn't see it. The streetlamps on the left side of the road were working. On the right side — eastbound — they weren't. Gerome was snoring aggressively in the backseat. After a while, Mark leaned his head against the passenger window.

"I'm just resting my eyes," he said.

Maggie turned down the radio.

"No, no," he said, his eyes already closed. "I promise not to fall asleep."

"Don't worry about it," Maggie said. "Rest."

"Just my eyes," he said. "I promise not to sleep."

He was out in five minutes. Maggie turned the radio off altogether. She liked the sound of the rain, the steady *thunk* of the wipers. She didn't necessarily like driving in weather like this, but at the end of the day, she didn't mind it. That's just how she was. And if Mark was tired, she was happy to let him sleep. He'd been working nonstop all semester. This was his break. It was time for him to rest up, to get his energy back so he could write.

The thing about Maggie: she would have made a good mom. People were always saying so. Her patients' owners especially couldn't believe she didn't have children. "But the way you are with animals . . ." It was a constant refrain.

Totally, totally, she'd thought about it. And why not? She was a woman: it was impossible not to have the discussion at some point or another. When they first started dating in fact, Mark had asked if she was interested, but the conversation hadn't lingered on babies. Instead, it turned quickly to Maggie's own mother. "There was so much disappointment in that house," she'd told him. "But there were also these photos, photos from before me and my brother, and in them my parents looked happy. I don't remember ever seeing them look happy around me." Maggie didn't think her parents' miserable attitudes were her fault, but she understood that — rightly or wrongly — she and her brother had changed things. "You know they didn't hug us?" she'd told Mark that day. "I can't remember a single hug. What I'm getting at, I suppose, is if it happens, it happens. But if it doesn't, I'll be okay." And it hadn't happened, and Maggie really was okay. There were bound to be regrets one day. When she was Gwen's age, for instance, she assumed she would experience a sort of homesickness for someone who never existed — a son, maybe a daughter. She'd miss the presence of youth in her life; miss getting to see that son or daughter fall in love for the first time. But Maggie also assumed that the homesickness would be infrequent, and the possibility of a future regret certainly didn't seem reason enough to change one's life now.

She slapped the steering wheel. "A mother," she said, though Mark was out cold, "what a strange thing to be." She shook her head.

Maggie glanced in the rearview. In the back, Gerome readjusted himself. His two yellow eyes glowed up at her. "Can you imagine?" she said to the dog. "Can you even imagine something so odd?"

Gerome sighed. The yellow eyes disappeared into the darkness of the backseat.

They were east of Xenia now, but they were no longer making good time. The rain had slowed everything down. At nearly every streetlight, she caught the red. They'd have to get a hotel eventually, but they wouldn't hit the big chains for another hour or two. They were still four hundred miles from Charlottesville, still two and a half hours from West Virginia.

"Damn it," Maggie said.

Mark shifted but didn't wake. The wipers ticked right, left, right, left. A streetlight ahead turned from green to yellow to red.

"Mark," she said.

He smacked his lips and yawned.

"Mark," she said again. Now she tapped him on the knee.

"We there?" His eyes were still closed.

She laughed. "You've been out twenty minutes," she said. "We're definitely not there."

"What's up?" He cracked his neck. He was slowly coming to.

"We didn't even think about dinner," she said.

US-35 was a wasteland when it came to food. Usually they were on 64, in West Virginia, by the time they were hungry, which meant Starbucks, Panera, Chipotle. US-35 involved gas stations with fried chicken and fast-food buffets with names like Krispy Kitchen and Fishin' Freddie's.

"Did you pack snacks?" he said.

She shook her head. "Only for Gerome."

The light turned green, and Maggie slowly pressed down on the gas.

"Don't get too close to the trucks," said Mark.

"I know," she said.

"Their brakes," he said.

She nodded. She wasn't annoyed. She might have been annoyed, but just then she wasn't. Just then she liked that he was acting a little paternal. It made her feel safe. It made her feel loved.

"How far are we from Charleston?" he said.

"Three hours," she said. "Then another three to Charlottesville."

Mark got out his phone.

"What are you looking at?" asked Maggie.

"Why are you always asking me that?"

"I didn't realize I was," she said.

"I'm checking e-mail."

"I thought you didn't like checking e-mail on your phone."

"Students," he said. "We left early. I want to make sure there are no questions about the final."

Mark was so meticulous about avoiding the computer at home. So meticulous, as a matter of fact, that lately she'd begun to wonder at it. Not that he could have known — because she wasn't in reality, as he'd suggested, always asking — but she'd recently grown curious about the nature of his online correspondence: computers, phones, or otherwise. For one thing, she'd been wondering why he changed his password a few months ago. That question had most certainly been on her mind, but no way had she brought it up with him. There were too many obvious follow-up inquiries from Mark:

1. How did she know he'd changed his password?
2. Had she tried logging in to his personal account?
3. His school account?
4. Why?

Surely — as far as he was concerned at least — his queries would trump and possibly invalidate her initial one: why had he needed to change it in the first place? So she hadn't asked, but it was something she wondered about from time to time.

"Also, I wanted to see where we are," he said, "on the map."

Mark had an early generation smartphone with a scratched-up screen; it was unlikely the map was even readable.

"Is it the stupidest idea in the world to say we should just turn around?" he said.

"Go back to Chicago?"

He gave a little chuckle. "Dayton," he said. "We're only twenty miles east of it."

"How is that even possible?" she said. "That makes no sense." It was daylight when they'd skirted Dayton. Now it was night.

"Small roads," he said. "Rain."

A station wagon pulled abruptly in front of them. Maggie hit the brakes and put her arm out as if to keep Mark from jerking forward. He took her hand and kissed it. "You're doing great," he said.

She smiled. "Thanks."

"Should we just keep going, then?" he said.

"I guess," she said. "The idea of Dayton ..."

"I know."

Mark went back to his phone. Maggie drove in silence for a few minutes, then turned on the radio. Mark turned it off again.

"Okay," he said. "Okay." He was looking at his screen. "We've got Washington Court House coming up and Chillicothe. There's got to be something there."

"You mean for the night?"

"No, no," he said. "Dinner. There must be something. Even if it's just a Subway. Then I'll be good to drive."

"You said we'd need a hotel."

"Eventually," he said. "But I think I can get us to West Virginia. It's not even eight yet. I can go another three hours for sure."

"Nine," she said.

"What?"

"It's nine," she said. "You're still on Chicago time."

He looked at his watch and then at his phone. "Damn," he said. "You're right."

"We'll hit the big hotels in an hour," she said. "We'll stop for the night then."

"It's not like they close," he said. "When we're ready, there will be something."

"It was your idea," she said. "Getting a hotel."

"It's fine," he said. "Promise. Let's make as much ground as we can. Short drive in the morning."

Obviously, in an ideal world, they wouldn't have to consider a hotel at all. But given the reports, given the state of the roads, a hotel was obviously the safest option. Only now that Maggie had come around to the idea, Mark was suddenly gung-ho to continue. Usually their timing was more in sync. She suspected, sadly, that he was trying to prove his masculinity in the most facile of ways: *I'm a man. Men drive through the night.*

Mark turned the radio back on and found the AM station, which was listing cities again.

"Let's eat soon, though," he said. "Whatever you see that looks good. Dinner's your call. I totally trust you."

All at once the rain doubled in its intensity. The station wagon ahead of them slammed on its brakes. Maggie did the same. They were jerked against their seat belts.

"Sorry," Maggie said. "I should be going even slower."

"There's no one I'd rather have beside me," he said.

"If you died, you mean?"

"If anything," he said. "Maybe put the hazards on, though. Until the rain lets up. Might as well."

She turned on the emergency lights.

Westbound, other cars followed suit one after the other, until soon the darkened highway seemed an uninterrupted stream of steady whites and blinking reds.

Maggie could no longer see the dotted lines of the road before her. Instead she leaned forward and concentrated on the milky water trails from the station wagon's tires.

"Dinner," she said, reducing her speed even more. "Sure. Fine. My choice."

And it was fine. Everything would be fine. Dinner in this neck of the woods would be a disappointment whatever they chose. But she'd take the fall. Mothers were always taking the fall. Sometimes it's just what they had to do to keep the family happy. True, Maggie wasn't an actual mother, but if you counted Gerome, they were an actual family. And sometimes women — whether they were mothers or not — just needed to take one for the team.

10

"Just park and I'll walk with you," Mark said.

"No point in both of us getting soaked," she said.

Maggie had pulled over at the curb of a squat brick building with neon cacti and sombreros in the windows.

"Seriously," he said. "Just park. We'll go in together."

The wipers, still hiked up to their fastest speed, went quiet when Maggie put the car in park, and now the front windshield was a streaming mess of water and neon.

"This is stupid," she said.

Gerome stood up in the backseat. He yawned.

"I'm not getting out without you," said Mark.

"Fine," she said.

The truth was he made her nervous when it came to parking. He should have just gotten out of the car like she wanted, but what kind of husband left his wife alone to park in the rain?

The lot was surprisingly full. Maggie circled it once, then twice, passing up two different empty spots.

"You hated those spaces?" Mark said.

She shook her head.

"There's one," he said. "Another one."

She was still shaking her head.

"You're mad?" he said.

"Stop talking," she said.

"Park," he said.

She slammed on the brakes. They were back at the curb.

"Get out," she said.

He laughed because it was ridiculous. "You get so worked up."

"You treat me like a child," she said.

"You act like a child."

"I'm not hungry anymore," she said.

Gerome gave a little yowl.

"Well, I am," Mark said. "So park the car."

He could see Maggie was on the brink of laughter but determined not to let it out. With his forefinger and thumb, he zipped his lips shut then swallowed an invisible key. She put the car into drive and did another lap.

"So you know," she said, "it's not that I think I can't park with you in the car."

He pointed to his lips and shrugged, eyes wide.

"I just want a spot where I can still see the car from inside," she said. "I want to be able to check on Gerome."

"You think someone is going to steal the dog?"

"I thought you swallowed the key," she said.

"In this weather?"

"So you didn't swallow the key," she said. "You were lying."

"I keep a spare in my pocket," he said.

In spite of herself, she laughed. "Should have known," she said.

A car backed out of a spot immediately outside the front windows of the restaurant. Maggie put on her turn signal and pulled in.

"I try to get mad and you turn instantly charming," she said. "I married a snake oil salesman."

"You break it, you buy it," he said, which was something she'd whispered to him on their wedding day. He'd never forgotten. It had become something they both said now and then — a way to acknowledge the fleas and ticks of their relationship, but also to acknowledge how good they had it: *Elizabeth and muggers be damned!* Or that was his take on the saying anyway. That's how he imagined she'd meant it when she said it the first time and how he meant it anytime he'd said it since.

"Gerome'll be fine," said Mark. He put a hand on her knee.

"He's just a dog after all," she said.

"That's right," he said.

"Just the world's best dog," she said.

They both turned inward in their seats to look at the dog. He was still standing, staring at them, dread in his eyes. He was just a dog, but he knew they were about to leave him in the car alone, the rain pounding the roof.

"Should we make a run for it?" Maggie said.

"Now or never."

Ten seconds later, they were standing under the canopy of a Mexican restaurant somewhere just east of Chillicothe. Mark's jeans were drenched. He looked down at Maggie. Her legs were glistening from the rain. He wanted to run his hands up and down them, an animal desire for ownership.

"You're a mess," he said. He felt suddenly lusty.

"Let's get inside."

They took a booth along the front windows, which were fogged. They could just barely make out their car and, inside, Gerome, who was still standing. But he'd give up in a minute or two and pass out. Then, when they returned, it would be like they'd never left at all.

77

Maggie scanned the menu. "Do you think this is safe?" she said. "Like, do you think we might get sick?"

Mark sighed. The Maggie he knew didn't ask questions about the safety of food. The Maggie he knew had made them go to Mexico for their honeymoon because she'd read about a no-kill shelter in need of supplies and thought it would be fun to do a little volunteering while they were supposed to be celebrating their marriage. "Just wait," she'd said. "Just wait and see how much more you enjoy life after you've done some good for no reason other than that you can." While they were down there, she'd eaten everything she could get her hands on — from a cart, from a trolley, from the back of a truck. Her digestive tract was indestructible. That was his Maggie. This one Mark wasn't so sure of.

"Do you know what you want?" he said.

"Do you want to split something?" She ran her finger up and down the page.

A waitress appeared.

Mark looked up. "What's good?" he said.

The waitress leaned toward him so that her cleavage was showing. She pressed her index finger onto his menu, next to a blurry picture of a plate piled high with food. "Spinach quesadilla," she said. "Popular."

When she removed her hand, the sweaty crosshatch of a fingerprint remained. With his thumb, Mark smeared the small grease stain away.

In the back of the restaurant — the kitchen, maybe — there was a small explosion, or what sounded like an explosion. The place went quiet. A few seconds later, the lights flickered. A few seconds after that, the lights went out altogether. The restaurant was pitch-black.

"Mark?" said Maggie.

"I'm right here," he said.

"Shh. Just wait." It was the waitress. She was whispering. She had leaned down even lower, her face close to their table. Mark thought he could feel her breath on his forehead, taste its salty foreignness in his mouth. His lustiness intensified and he pushed himself down into his seat. He considered sucking his thumb. "Just wait one second," she said. "The electrical panel. It's been popping all night."

A minute later there was the sound of another small explosion, and then the lights were back. Then, a moment after that, a sound system started up, the televisions behind the bar powered back on, and the place filled with a sort of Mexican ska that hadn't been playing before. The other diners — who Mark now realized must have been moderately to very drunk — cheered. The waitress beamed. "Told you," she said. But it wasn't addressed to them so much as it was to the pad in her hand and the people around them.

Mark looked at Maggie. She was sitting dead still, her posture perfect, her lips pressed together so that he couldn't see that cherished gap. Her shoulders were high and tensed. Her immediate atmosphere had gone cold.

"Maybe we need a minute?" Maggie said. "I'm not ready to order yet." She was looking at Mark, imploring him with her big eyes. What they were saying — her big doe eyes — was, *Let's get out of here, let's go right now, let's leave before there's trouble and we all wind up dead, dead, dead.* But he couldn't do it. He was tired. He needed some food and maybe a quick beer to help with the tension in his knees.

The waitress — petite, dark-skinned — was still standing there. She didn't have the body type or facial features that, twenty years ago, Mark would have found attractive. But now, a middle-aged man, he was able to see the appeal in the roundness of such a jaw, the fullness of such a thigh.

"One Corona," he said.

"What are you doing?" said Maggie. "I thought you were driving next."

"I am," he said to Maggie. To the waitress he said, "And a lime."

The waitress wrote it down. She didn't care about Mark and Maggie or who was driving next. For that matter, neither did she care about the jumpy electric panel in back or the encroaching storm outside. What she cared about was the tip jar and her next shot of tequila and her two or three little babies waiting for her at home. What she cared about had nothing to do with them, and for that — for her supreme, nearly palpable indifference — Mark felt his entire heart open up.

11

When the waitress brought a third beer, Maggie reached for it before Mark could. She took a long, slow swig.

"Ten-thirty," the waitress said, putting a bill on the table. "Closing time."

The rain had stopped. The window they sat next to was bulleted by the occasional sheet of wind, but other than that, it seemed perhaps the worst of this particular storm might have passed. Gerome hadn't raised his head — not that Maggie had seen from where they were still sitting in the booth — in at least a half hour.

It wasn't so much that Maggie minded the idea of having a drink and then getting back in the car. In fact, one of her favorite things to do in Virginia, in Mark's home state, was drink and drive on the small back roads that zigzagged between farmland and country life. She loved the freedom of it, the thrill of an open container combined with a curving flat road late at night. But this wasn't a quiet private lane in Virginia they were talking about. This was a full-scale road trip. This was a late-at-night, middle-of-nowhere drive across five states, and the idea of adding booze to the equation just seemed thick. It hadn't been her idea, but there was no going back now.

She took another slow swig. Her mugger had been drunk. She'd smelled it on his breath, in his clothes. He'd been at a bar, some place that still let regulars and old-timers smoke inside. She often thought about which bar it might have been — was it a place close to where they lived? She wondered whether or not he still went there. Sometimes, lately, she wondered if he'd been too drunk to remember her the next day or if, even now, even still, he thought about her from time to time. Her hand trembled slightly. She didn't like the idea of that man out there, existing, conjuring her up whenever he wanted.

She closed her eyes, took another drink, and tried not to think of the coed. She would finish this beer and still be fine enough to deliver them to the closest hotel, which was no longer up for debate: getting a hotel was now a must.

Funny how she'd come 180 degrees in just one day. That morning you couldn't have paid her to consider stopping, but now, in this weather, alcohol in her blood *and* in Mark's? She'd sooner chew off her own hands than try to make the Blue Ridge tonight.

They'd have to start looking immediately. They were a half hour from Jackson, an hour from Gallipolis. They'd pass probably a half-dozen hotels in that hour. Not the best places, but one of them would get the job done. No problem. She'd check them in, walk Gerome by herself just to show Mark that she could — there was a small canister of mace in a zippered pocket of her purse — then she'd shower, slip into bed, pass out. She'd put this day behind her.

In the morning she'd wake up and they'd be halfway to Virginia. The storm would be a thing of the past, and everything could just go back to normal. On Monday she'd have Gwen saddle up one of the older mares for her, and she'd make a routine of it while they were at the farm. She'd get some riding in, go for regular runs in the mornings. Maybe she'd drive into town with Robert, hit a few golf balls at the country club with him if he didn't mind. The club had only recently let women on the course, and she wasn't sure how Robert felt about that. But she'd suss him out, and if all was copacetic, she'd hit some balls with him. Ten years ago she'd had a decent swing, or so Mark had told her.

The important thing — once they got to Virginia — was that she leave Mark alone. And that Mark, for a little while at least, leave her alone. They needed some time. Not *away* from each other exactly, but to themselves. And being with his family would allow them both some breathing room. It might be a strange thing for a daughter-in-law to admit, but Maggie genuinely looked forward to these trips, to his parents. They had a way of pampering her to just the right degree. All the love she never felt from her own parents, she felt from his. She drank up their attention. Plus, it was always so nice not to have to walk Gerome on a leash. That was something she always looked forward to, seeing him romp, watching his elegant vaults over the log jump-course near the lavender fields where Gwen sometimes worked the horses. He really was a beautiful dog.

It occurred to Maggie — as she watched Mark pull his wallet from his pants pocket — that he might want to have sex when they finally got to the hotel. Nothing turned Mark on more than a night in a strange place. Maggie shuddered at the thought. Don't get her wrong: she was still attracted to him. Of course she was! He had a beautiful head of hair. She liked to run her hand through it, grab a small fistful, then lean in close for a deep inhale. He had zero belly fat, but not in an obsessive caveman way. He was, in her honest and unbiased estimation, a visually perfect specimen of a real and total man. She'd marry him all over again for his looks alone. Probably every one of his students had crushes. Textbook scenario: If they were girls, they wanted to date him; if they were boys, they wanted to be him. But who cared about students? Mark was hers.

Lately, though — and this was a phenomenon she was still puzzling out — she'd been turned off by the idea of sex in bed. It felt too intimate, too serious. Instead, she found herself increasingly turned on when, for instance, driving to get groceries. Or finishing up her day's notes at the clinic. Walking the dog, perhaps. Taking an elevator or brushing her teeth. She hadn't told Mark about her recent change in appetite. Not that she could guess his reaction. Maybe he'd be equally turned on by her admission; maybe he wouldn't. But she was worried by the possibility that he'd somehow find a way to take the change personally, which was the last thing she wanted. And so she'd kept her desires to herself, which meant recently there hadn't been as much sex as either of them would have liked. She had considered more than once bringing it up with her former therapist, but she could never settle on an appropriate opening.

Mark slid out of the booth with the tab in his hand and walked away. A moment later he was back.

"Do you have any cash?" he said.

"I have a couple hundreds in the car," she said.

"Nothing smaller?"

"No," she said. "Sorry. Just use the card."

He shook his head. "No can do."

"Why?"

He was avoiding eye contact. Never a good sign with Mark.

"Why?" she said again. She kept her voice steady, her gaze easy.

"The system is down," he said.

"The system?"

"They've been running on a generator for the last fifteen minutes."

Maggie looked out the window. She couldn't see Gerome, which meant either he'd been taken — which of course he hadn't, she wasn't a complete nitwit — or he was conked out. She looked back up at Mark, who was still standing there, looking down at the bill.

"What does that mean?" she said. "There's power. We have power here."

"No," he said. "They're offline. Everything is offline. The entire town is dark."

"But —" Maggie looked again out the window. She looked this time past the car, past the parking lot. She looked into the deep expanse of darkness where golden bulbs at various heights and of incalculable degrees of intensity should have been twinkling and blinking and bright. What she realized was that the entirety of 35 was black. Not a single streetlamp was illuminated.

12

They'd been back on the road for maybe ten minutes. Twenty max. They'd passed two hotels, both with their NO VACANCY signs lit up. Maggie thought there was power, but Mark explained it only meant more generators. Anyway, these were piece-of-shit places. Tiny holes-in-the-wall right on the highway like the Piney Inn Motel, or whatever it was. And neither Mark nor Maggie had even suggested they stop and make sure there wasn't a room. Maggie had offered to keep driving when they left the restaurant. She'd made a little show of it in fact: "Just give me the keys. I've had fewer than you." But Mark insisted he take over. She wouldn't admit it, not to him, but the beer had gotten her tipsy. Her tolerance was essentially nonexistent. She said she was acting funny only because she was tired, but Mark knew better.

He glanced over at her, thinking she'd be passed out. But her eyes were open and she was looking down at her lap.

"What are you doing?"

"Reading," she said. She waved her phone at him.

"What about?"

"Do you really want to know?"

Gerome was snoring. When they got back in the car, he didn't even wake up. It could have been anybody up there in the front seats and Gerome wouldn't have known the difference.

"It's hard to concentrate with you over there reading," he said.

"Does the light bother you?"

The light didn't bother him. There was hardly any light at all coming from her little device. She'd turned the screen glow down. She was considerate like that.

"Fine," he said. "Sure. Hit me. Read me something."

Maggie turned the radio off. They'd been listening to modern country by default.

"Okay," she said. "A group of teenagers — high school students — kidnap a college kid and torture him to death."

"No," he said. "Not that. Try again."

"Okay," said Maggie. She was quiet for a minute. "This is the story of a young woman who discovers her father has been videotaping her every time he rapes her, and it turns out she's essentially famous in the world of Internet pedophilia. Like, the most famous molested girl in the world."

"Jesus," he said. "No." Where was she getting this stuff? He read the same papers she did. But he never came across articles like those. Or, if he did, he had enough sense to skip over them. "I don't want to hear about children getting hurt. Anything other than children getting hurt."

"Okey-doke." Maggie poked at her screen. "How about this? Google has issued a statement."

They were always issuing statements — the big companies — and always about the smallest things. They were afraid they'd be forgotten if they didn't constantly update or reload.

"What kind of statement?"

"Their maps department is going to stop removing dead bodies from satellite images."

Mark had no idea what she was talking about.

"I can read you the article," she said.

"Maybe just a summary?" he said. "Maybe just the bare bones?"

Maggie was quiet a moment. He could see from the corner of his eye that she was looking at her lap again. Her index finger flicked vertically at her phone.

"Okay," she said. "It's an apology-slash-statement."

Of course it was.

"They set a precedent several years ago by removing that boy's body in Texas, and they're saying now that it was the wrong precedent to have set. They're saying now that it's impossible to remove all the bodies because there are too many."

"What boy's body in Texas?"

"They're saying that the last hurricane makes it a precedent they can no longer live up to and — this is verbatim — *nor do we wish to continue to erase the realities of our planet's surface.* Can you believe that?"

No. He couldn't believe it.

He couldn't believe that such a thing existed. Why were there photos at all? Why was there a maps department at Google that had any authority to issue statements in the first place? Hadn't the world gotten along perfectly fine before satellite imaging? Did your everyday housewife really require access to professional-grade topological views of the earth? To the Internet at all? Jesus, just look at Maggie since the mugging, since the college girl. Look how quickly she'd gone from simple browser to consummate addict.

"Burglaries are up on the North Side," Maggie said. "Want to hear about that?"

"Go for it."

"And sexual assaults."

It was exhausting — not Maggie, but the news itself. Lately — and this was something that didn't make him happy, didn't secretly fill him with joy — the two felt fused together. Maggie was the news and the news was Maggie. He missed his wife.

"A decade ago," she was saying, "the theory was that men who raped were motivated differently from men who mugged. So you could get mugged and not worry about getting raped."

"Are you reading this?" said Mark. "Or is this you talking?" He didn't like to take his eyes off the road, especially with it being so late and the weather being so unpredictable, but he was fairly certain she was going off book with all this.

A commercial truck came into view on the near side of the westbound lanes. Mark flashed his brights. The truck responded by turning on its high beams.

"Christ," said Mark, squinting.

Maggie didn't say anything.

"I thought his brights were on," he said.

Maggie still didn't say anything.

The truck passed. Mark rubbed his eyes, and again it was just them and their own headlights and the occasional streetlamp.

"Anyway," said Maggie. "Now muggers are rapists, and rapists are muggers. There's no distinction. Terrorists are mass murderers, and school shooters are terrorists. Et cetera. Et cetera." She was definitely off book. This was her brain. This was unfiltered Maggie trying to sew together bits and pieces of millions of different articles. This was Maggie hoping to make sense of a world in which she could be mugged by one man and then, nine months later, a neighbor could be raped and murdered by another. Two women. Two men. Two entirely different outcomes but somehow — improbably, unfairly — they both, Maggie and the college girl, wound up with nearly identical bruises on the backs of their necks. Only Maggie was still alive and her bruise had healed. Whereas now the college girl was dead and her bruise ... had done whatever bruises did when people died. "If you can steal a wallet," Maggie was saying, "why not also steal a fuck?"

Mark shook his head. For starters, he didn't like when she profaned. It wasn't natural. Sure, he had a bit of a sailor's mouth himself, that was true — and his students adored him for it — but on her, it sounded dirty. It sounded adolescent and unearned. But that wasn't even the point. The point was she was wrong about murderers being muggers and muggers being rapists. He knew she was wrong, but it wasn't worth it. It wasn't worth starting an argument that might last until morning. There was no way they were going to make it to the Blue Ridge tonight. They needed a hotel — sooner than later, actually, since his eyes were getting heavy — and the thought of being in a little shithole with his wife while they were both still stewing over some half-baked argument ... Well, the thought made him want to weep.

"I'm good," he said. "Thanks. No more articles for me, okay?"

He patted her thigh like he might pat Gerome's head. "Can you find me a new channel? Anything other than country."

"Do you just want silence?"

"No," he said. "I want to hear something." He didn't like the idea of sitting there listening to her read to herself.

Maggie put her phone down and attended to the radio. She flipped through a few stations.

"Wait," he said. "Go back."

She went back.

"Stop," he said. "There."

"This?"

A man was talking. He had the telltale conviction of an evangelist.

"Yes," he said. "Perfect."

Maggie was looking at him. He could feel her face like a full moon in his periphery.

"You're actually interested in listening to this man?" she said. On the radio, the voice was explaining away dinosaurs and fossilization with Noah's flood.

"You don't think it's fascinating?"

Mark really did get a kick out of these people. To him, it was mesmerizing the way they rewrote history, working themselves into little frenzies over the most trivial things as they went along. Just then, for instance, the voice was telling the story of early settlers, who had apparently interviewed Indians — their words — who had apparently spoken of dinosaurs as a recent memory! The idea of Christians using the word of Indians as their proof — it was delightful. Utterly delightful! If only Maggie could find the humor in it, as she once, not too long ago, certainly would have.

"Fine," Maggie said. "You win."

She leaned her head against the window and closed her eyes.

"Win nothing," he said. "It's not a competition."

But lately — and this was the unhappy, undesired state of their current condition — it *was* a competition.

What was the joke his father was always telling about what happens when you play a country song backward? *You get your dog back, your wife back, your life back . . . ?* Well, that's exactly what Mark wanted back now: his Maggie, his marriage. *Goddamn it!* His life — as he'd once so transcendently been living it — he wanted it back!

13

The first thing Maggie was aware of was her open mouth. She licked her lips, then ran her tongue along her gum lines until they were moist again.

The second thing she was aware of was a soreness at the base of her neck. She sat up, rolled her shoulders forward and back, back and forward. She opened and closed her mouth, re-licked her lips.

It was quiet in the car and dark, and it took her a minute to realize she wasn't in the driveway of Mark's parents' farm. In the early days, such things were possible. In the twelfth hour of the drive, Maggie could switch to the passenger seat, rest her head against the window for what she believed was merely a moment, then fall into a sleep so heavy, so deep that Mark would be unable to rouse her when they pulled into his parents' gravel drive. He'd been forced more than once to leave her there, in the passenger seat, until she woke on her own, usually close to morning, the neighbors' roosters her alarm. But this was before. This was long ago. This was back when sleep came fast and easy no matter where she was. They could pop in a video in the early days of their marriage, and she'd be out cold in ten minutes. Mark hadn't been miffed by it. He'd been, in fact, overjoyed. He used to say how good it made him feel — that his wife found such comfort in their life together that she could sleep through anything. She'd always liked this assessment of her patterns. She'd been as captivated by the idea as he. But in this last year, sleep had turned obstinate; the silence of the bedroom and the dark of midnight had become something to dread. In reexamining her relationship with the dark, she'd stumbled accidently onto a question she hadn't intended ever to consider: Did not the difficulty of sleep necessarily suggest a departure of the intense confidence she'd once had in her home life?

She cleared her throat.

This wasn't the time to pursue such dreary considerations because she was not now in Mark's parents' gravel driveway, where she should have been. Instead, she was — she realized as her eyes adjusted — in a parking lot, in the passenger seat of their car, alone. Almost alone. Gerome was in the back, sleeping. She could hear him breathing.

The parking lot was unlit. She looked up and out the sunroof. Above the car — she could just barely make it out — was a streetlamp, but the streetlamp was dead.

She checked the door. Hers was unlocked. She sat up a little straighter and then checked the driver's side and the backseat. Also unlocked. She didn't want to panic, but she did want to scream. Anger, fear, fatigue: Who could say for sure what she was feeling. All of them? None of them? She was simultaneously filled up with and emptied out of emotions. She thought about hitting the glove compartment, but that would be a punishment only to her hand. And the thing she wanted to punish — the person who had abandoned her in an unlocked car in the middle of nowhere — was currently and conveniently MIA.

She did the next best thing to hitting and screaming. She closed her eyes, clenched her fists, gritted her teeth, and visualized her own skull exploding. She imagined little pieces of cranium sticking to the upholstery of the roof, sliding down the inside of the windshield. Protoplasmic fibers splattered against the rearview mirror. Chunks of cerebellum landed on the dashboard. Her medulla dangled limply from the passenger headrest. She stayed like this until she heard a tiny buzzing at the base of her brain, and then she released herself. Except, she wasn't released. Because now her heartbeat was racing, which necessarily engaged her anxiety, and she found herself suddenly clawing at the lock button in a sloppy and erratic sort of way that reminded her out of nowhere of climbing up a pool ladder when, as a child, she'd once managed to convince herself — though she knew it to be a pure impossibility — that piranhas had materialized in the deep end.

She pushed the button. The sound of the doors sealing themselves against the night filled the car with a hollow *thwunk*. Gerome stirred, but nothing more.

In the glove compartment there was a tin candy box the size of a matchbook. In this tin candy box there was a mixture of square-shaped breath mints and circular yellow pills. She took a deep breath and exhaled the air slowly. She did not reach for the box. Her former therapist had trained her well enough so that she didn't need to take one every time her nerves clicked on. Sometimes — like now — it was enough just to know they were there. Lemon-colored ellipsoids interspersed neatly with small white squares. It was enough just to imagine them and all the good they could do to her central nervous system if she so chose.

Also in the compartment was an emergency first-aid kit. Its contents were geared more toward animals than humans — large bandages, strong sedatives, at least one legal barbiturate — and not at all toward practical survival, which meant there wasn't a flashlight, which was the only thing Maggie truly wanted at that moment.

She cracked her neck. She was starting to notice other things about her current situation. The car key, for starters, was not in the ignition — she felt for it, just to be sure — nor was it in the center console, and the car itself was warm. In fact, the car was very warm, and she was warm, and Gerome — now she heard it more distinctly — wasn't just snoring; he was panting. Mark had left the two of them in an unlocked car, in the middle of the night, in the middle of nowhere, in the middle of a heat wave. It was possible he'd finally lost his mind.

She reached behind her seat and pulled out a half-filled water bottle. She took a sip and then poured a little into her cupped palm. She wiped it onto the fur under Gerome's ear and then around his neck. Gerome moaned and flipped himself gently so that his belly was exposed. She poured a little bit more onto her hand — she dared Mark to say something about the leather; she just dared him — and then rubbed it along his abdomen. Gerome stretched, but still he made no move to stand. She put the back of her hand under his chin. His heartbeat was fast, but he was fine. This was simply a dog's body's way of cooling itself.

At least Gerome wasn't dying back there. At least he wasn't dead because —

And then for a half second — no, less than a half second, a nanosecond, a piece of time so fleeting there's no way truly to prove it ever existed except through the memory of the thought — Maggie imagined the satisfaction she might feel if Gerome had a heat stroke and died. She imagined the permanent regret with which Mark would be forever saddled. She imagined the upper hand she would have for the rest of their lives. But then immediately — almost immediately, because the nanosecond exists and existed — she felt intense guilt for having used the fantasy of Gerome's death as a way to inflict a make-believe punishment on her husband. Dear god, she was turning perverse. Maybe there *was* something irreversibly wrong with her.

She wanted to roll down a window or crack the door, but she couldn't risk exposing herself. She leaned forward, cupped a hand to the windshield, and looked out. The parking lot was full of empty cars and trucks — or what she assumed were empty cars and trucks. Who knows? Maybe the lot was filled with women in similar situations — women lousy with despair, lousy with anxiety; women stifled by the heat and by their fear and by their own lousy husbands. Ha! If only there were other women in the night . . .

Imagine the things they could say to one another . . .

Imagine the stories they could tell . . .

Imagine the comfort they might feel to be so safely ensconced in such a large number of the same sex . . .

But there were no other women.

There were only cars and trucks. And they were all parked, just as theirs was, in what appeared to be a large paved ravine surrounded on all sides by tall dirt banks. Maggie gazed higher and, doing so, noticed that, in the distance, up and beyond the dirt walls, there was light. A muted glowing light. Pale and lemony, just like her pills.

14

"All I mean," said Mark, "is that it makes no sense."

He was standing in the lobby of the sixth hotel he'd walked into since Maggie had passed out in the passenger seat. Not a vacancy at a single one of them.

The man behind the counter said nothing. He was a kid really, not a man, though his hairline was already receding.

They were both sweating.

"Listen," said Mark. The kid looked hopelessly inbred, which probably accounted for his hairline. Bad genes. Bad genes combined with more bad genes. "I get that I seem like a dick right now."

"Can you mind your language?" the kid said. He looked back and forth like it was study hall and any second they'd get caught. "There are children here." He gestured down the hallway, at the end of which was a large glass wall, fogged and dirty and behind which was an indoor pool. Mark could hear the splashes of water, the cackling of children and adults.

"Shouldn't the pool be closed?" Mark said. "Aren't there hours for things like that?" He didn't mean it as an accusation. He was curious, that was all. But given how the last few minutes had been going, Mark could handily see how his questions might be misinterpreted as aggressive, especially by an inbred.

The clerk sighed. He was growing weary of Mark's presence. "We don't have the a/c back yet." He shook his head and let his arms fall to his sides. "The generators give us light and electricity for fans and toasters, but we don't have the a/c."

Fans and toasters. Mark nodded. "And you also don't have rooms even though the sign outside says you do?"

"Sir, like I said —" But the clerk was interrupted by the abrupt appearance at Mark's side of a small wet child, naked but for an inner tube.

"Mama says to come right now," the child said.

There was no greeting, no salutation, no apology, no *Excuse me* or *May I step in for a moment?* The inner tube squeaked against the child's skin, which glistened under the fluorescents.

"Mama says it's important there's something wrong with the pool and can you come now."

Maggie would have been able to say for certain how old the child was, but Mark was at a loss. Anything old enough to speak full sentences should probably not have been naked in public. And yet here this child was. Mark put his hands in his pockets. He felt vaguely culpable — like after a dream in which he'd perhaps cheated on Maggie with a faceless woman or, being completely honest, a woman with Elizabeth's face. A crime. But not a crime.

"Mama says right now okay that's what Mama says."

The clerk sighed again. Between Mark and the naked child, there was no clear winner, but the child was a guest and Mark was not, and that seemed to settle things.

"Sir," said the clerk, but moving toward the child, already sidling away from Mark and in the direction of the pool. "I'm sorry about the Vacancy sign. I'm sorry you were confused. The generator is picking and choosing tonight. You're not the first. If it makes any difference. We've been disappointing people all night."

The child was already running across the carpet, leading the way for the clerk. Unwittingly, Mark observed the boy's heels, on the backs of which were loose and blackened bandages. As the boy trotted, they flapped against his skin.

Mark slumped forward onto the counter so that his face was immediately in front of a small portable fan. He had nothing to show for his effort and no one to berate or blame for the lack of available rooms. He thought of Maggie and Gerome. He hoped they were both still asleep. He'd wanted to return valiant. He'd wanted to do right by them both — return to the car with a key in his hand, wake Maggie with a kiss to the forehead, which would fill her with feelings of kindness and warmth, which, in turn, even from the backseat, Gerome would sense and — inexplicably to the dog — cause him to feel a sudden rush of affection and wonderful subservience for his male master.

Without raising his head, Mark looked at his watch. It was almost one in the morning and he was spent. Perhaps he could move the car from the lower lot to the upper one, where they'd at least be under the light of the hotel and its generator. He could leave the car running, blast the a/c until the sun came up. He only needed a few hours of rest.

He closed his eyes and let the fan blow into his face.

"Fuck," he said. "Double fuck."

"Sir?"

It was the clerk again, who'd returned without the child.

"Sorry," said Mark. He stood and moved the fan away, as though returning the breeze he'd only temporarily borrowed. "Really, I am. I didn't mean — We're just beat, that's all. Dead beat."

The kid appeared not to have heard him. He was acting

101

twitchy, nervous even. Perhaps one of the hotel's paying customers had left a turd in the deep end. Perhaps the clerk was worried
it would fall on him to retrieve the thing.

Mark turned to leave. But the kid put a hand on his.

"I know a place," he said.

Mark looked down at the narrow fingers on top of his own.
They were speckled with eczema.

The kid was whispering, and he'd leaned in toward the counter and toward Mark so that now the portable fan blew the blond
wisps of what was left of the kid's hair up and away from his scalp.
Caterpillar scabs inched across the hairline.

"What I mean is, I can't recommend other hotels. It being policy and all. But my brother-in-law's got a place up in Black Crows
Hill, and I know for a fact they still had rooms an hour ago. Lots
of 'em."

Mark hadn't heard of Black Crows Hill before, which meant it
couldn't be on 64. But perhaps it was close. A little townlet just a
few miles from the interstate.

"Could you give me directions?" Already Mark could feel himself the hero. His fantasy wasn't an impossibility after all. He pic-
tured himself walking back to the car, starting the ignition in such
a way as to not wake Maggie, and delivering them to a mountainside gem with a generator and running water and clean cool
sheets.

"Policy says . . ." the clerk trailed off.

"Please," said Mark. He knew he sounded frantic. Then, thinking perhaps of the wet child or the unsavory feel of the clerk's
hand on his or the idea of inbreeding and incest in general or
maybe simply because he missed Maggie at that moment, missed
her savagely and needed to invoke her presence, the idea of her
presence, needed to confirm her mere existence in his life, Mark
said, out of nowhere, "My wife — my wife and I both — we really

appreciate anything more you can tell me. The name"— he was whispering now, hoping to show his respect for the policy —"just give me the name, and I'll find it on my own." He held the clerk's gaze. "Please."

For a moment, the clerk just stood there, a possible mute. Mark thought he could hear the ticking of a wall clock from somewhere behind the desk, but the ticking was too lazy, too irregular to be marking time precisely.

Slowly, the boy raised a hand to his mouth, as if to stifle a yawn. The ticking continued. Then, nearly inaudibly, the hand still covering his mouth, he said, "Holiday Inn."

"Holiday Inn?" said Mark. He stood up straighter. There was no way there was a major hotel that wasn't already filled to capacity. The storm — though it had essentially quieted down — had left a bona fide, governor- declared disaster zone in its wake. Just as his parents had predicted it would.

"No," said the clerk, nearly hissing now. "Holi*days* Inn."

"With an *s*?" said Mark.

"With an *s*," he said. "Like lots of holidays."

Mark nodded. Of course. Lots of holidays. Every holiday. It was perfect. Simply perfect. He nearly shrieked with laughter. A mongoloid hotel with a mongoloid name in a mongoloid town. Maggie would die. She would just die.

Mark didn't even say thank you. Didn't even need to. The clerk was already on his way back to the pool.

Their automobile was gone.

This wasn't possible.

Mark was standing next to the streetlamp beneath which he'd earlier parked the car, the car in which Maggie and Gerome had been sleeping. And, here — right here — just where he was standing now, was the very same Wagoneer he'd parked next to. Here were its long dented doors and backyard paint job. He recalled like it was still happening the decision to park next to the Wagoneer despite its ratty appearance because it was the middle of the night and its owners were probably already in bed, probably fast asleep, but more importantly because it was a spot beneath a streetlight. Though the streetlight hadn't been illuminated, he remembered thinking, *In case the power comes back. In case. If Maggie wakes, there will be light.* Here the Wagoneer was and here Mark was, but the spot in which their car had been was empty.

He checked his front pocket. The keys to the car were still there. Next he reached for his phone but — *fuck* — he'd left it in the car. He put his hands on his head; he was about to start thinking all the worst thoughts. He was about to take a page from Maggie's book and let his imagination run wild, but just then a car across the lot turned its headlights on. Mark put a hand to his eyes. The car's brights flashed — on then off then on again.

It was their car.

It was Maggie.

He trotted across the lot, still using his hand to shield his eyes from the high beams.

She was in the driver's seat, laughing.

"What the fuck, Maggie?" he said. "Jesus Christ. I thought — I don't know what I thought."

She rolled down the window and looked up at him, completely unconcerned. "I used the spare," she said. "Thank god I remembered it. Gerome nearly had a stroke."

Mark looked in the back at Gerome who, though lying down, was awake and alert to — if not completely interested in — the action around him.

"The GPS is broken," said Maggie. She knocked on the screen

at the center of the dash. "Or not working. Or something." She knocked a few more times. "Worthless."

"What were you thinking?" said Mark. He was still standing at the driver's-side window, still looking in at his wife. "Were you trying to be funny? Moving the car?" He could feel himself getting angry. Or, rather, he felt the right to be angry, to get angry, if necessary.

"The question is what were *you* thinking?" she said. "You left us in a parking lot in the middle of nowhere."

"We're not in the middle of nowhere."

"With the doors unlocked."

"With the doors un—" Mark stopped himself. He couldn't believe it. After everything he'd been trying to do for her. While she was comfortably asleep. After the six hotels and the imbecilic desk clerks, after all that, she wasn't even a little bit thankful? She wasn't grateful? Why was he surprised? She was exactly as she'd been for the past three weeks: scared. And scared, he was realizing now, perhaps for the very first time, of *everything*. That was it. He was finally starting to see. It wasn't just nighttime; it wasn't just the man in the alley and the man in the college girl's apartment. She hadn't simply turned scared of the dark. She'd turned scared of life.

"But Gerome is here," he said at last. "You were completely safe, Maggie. You must see that?" He felt on the brink of despair; felt very close to losing respect for his wife forever. *Please,* he thought. *Please don't be as nuts as I think you might actually be.* He was lonely in an adolescent way, like he was the last one on the playground, his mother not yet arrived and even the janitor gone for the night. He felt helpless and, god, he felt utterly alone.

Maggie stuck her arm out the window and took his hand. Was she reading his mind?

"Yes," she said. "I do see that. I do, which is why I thought I'd have a bit of fun. Come here." She pulled at his hand, and he bent down to the window. "Kiss me."

He kissed her—nothing dramatic or drawn out, but a real kiss, lip against lip. They both smelled of salt and sweat.

"At first," she said, while he was still bent low, still close to her face. "At first I was mad. Then I was scared. Then I was embarrassed for being scared. Then I remembered the key. Then I realized that all of it—my moodiness—was because I was so bloody hot, and then Gerome and I thought it would be funny to move the car—he peed, by the way—and then we called your mom."

Mark stood up. Gerome peed? He looked around the lot. But that would mean that Maggie had walked him. Alone. In the dark. In the middle, as she'd said herself, of nowhere. He had a strong desire to congratulate her, to thank her for being so normal, but he worried that to acknowledge it, to point directly at the thing he was so happy for, might make it retreat, might send it scurrying—a newly frightened kitten—under the belly of the car for good.

"You called Gwen?"

"We woke her up."

He looked at his watch. One a.m. exactly. "I would think so," he said. "Yes."

Overhead, there was a large crack of thunder. Mark ducked, then straightened and appraised the night sky. A waning crescent was very briefly visible but a wind was moving fast and soon, while he stood there watching in fact, the moon was lost to cloud cover. He held his hand out, palm up. No rain. Not yet.

"Get in the car," said Maggie. "I'll tell you all about it."

"I'll drive," he said. He opened Maggie's door and held out his hand; she took it. Gerome watched as Mark patted her on the butt and pushed her around to the passenger's side.

When they were both in the car, Maggie hit the lock button. "Just for fun," she said, poking Mark's knee. "But look." She held up her phone. "I can't get Internet, but I can access the map from the last time it loaded and we can see just enough of the county to get us where we're going."

Now there was lightning over the hotel — a majestic tree branch illuminating the building and its upper packed parking lot.

"It's not done after all," Maggie said.

"What are you talking about?"

"The storm," she said. "There are about four different systems that Gwen says we'll be darting in and out of."

And now there was thunder and lightning together, and the interior of the car was lit up momentarily. Mark's hands glowed purple and ghostly on the steering wheel.

Maggie turned to the backseat. Gerome hadn't moved. "He's being so good," she said. "Because you're back now."

"But what were you talking about before?" said Mark. "Where are we going? What do you mean?"

"Gwen got online and found a place."

"With rooms?"

"She booked it and everything."

Mark was confused. All this time he'd been inside that dump trying, and halfway succeeding, to find them a refuge, and meanwhile Maggie — the woman he'd been so quick to call a loser, the woman he'd thought had forgotten how to function on her own — had been outside making it happen. Yes, sure, with the help of his mother, but still. He put his hands on Maggie's face.

"Woman," he said. He wanted to press into her skin until she could feel his relief in her cheekbones.

Only three days ago Elizabeth had ended her e-mail with a question: "So what is she, the love of your life?" It was the first time the circumstance of his marriage had ever been mentioned in writing, and he'd deleted it without writing back, troubled that he'd allowed his wife to become fodder for a younger woman's flirtation. He'd been frightened by the question, frightened by his own hesitancy. And yet, just now, his hands on either side of Maggie's face, Mark felt confident that it was within his grasp to give up this minor obsession. Elizabeth was nothing. He'd always known. But now he felt supremely and safely sure.

"Man," Maggie said.

She seemed not to mind that he was pressing so hard. He pressed harder still.

"*My* woman," he said.

"My *man*," she said, and now she smiled, and — *god!* — that smile, that wonderful gap between her teeth. It gave him the same high happiness he'd felt early on in their courtship when a grin or a giggle from Maggie could turn him kingly and strong.

"I don't know if it's dog-friendly," she said, shaking her face free of his hands finally. "But I doubt they'll be too particular. Gwen tried calling. No one's answering but that's hardly a surprise. Still, that they have Internet and that we could book must be a good sign. They'll have a generator at the very least."

Mark kissed her on the forehead and turned up the a/c. He gestured toward the map on the phone. "You'll be my guide?"

And now the rain did start, the slightest sweetest bit of water hitting the windshield and trickling slowly down the glass in Tourettic lines.

"Seat belt," Maggie said. She pinched his shirt where it covered a nipple.

He did as instructed. He liked that she could still be bossy, even in a cute, unimposing way, even about such a frivolous thing. It reminded him of Elizabeth, which was something he'd have to stop letting himself do: be reminded so easily of Elizabeth.

"You'll never guess what the place is called," she said. "Never in a million years. Gwen and I had quite a laugh."

Mark put the car in gear and — only after Maggie had indicated the way — steered them toward the exit.

"Holidays Inn?" Mark said. "With an *s*?"

Maggie slapped her knee. "Yes!"

"Like lots of holidays?" he said.

"How did you know?"

"You wouldn't believe me," said Mark.

Now Maggie pointed at the entrance to the interstate. "Take a right here. We get back on, but only for twenty or so miles. Then it's all boonies and backwoods for this car."

Mark took the turn.

"I just about died when Gwen told me the name," Maggie said, and for the first time all day — for the first time maybe all year and certainly in the past three weeks — Mark felt that the two of them were in exactly the same place, at exactly the same moment, experiencing everything in exactly the same way.

15

And now a pause. A breath. A moment away. Leave the car. Just open the door and step out. Stretch if you must. Stand on the tips of your toes, bend your knees, jump skyward, toward the moon — the little that's illuminated. Don't worry about your skin. You have no skin here. This is only the imagination — its senses — that's taking this flight. Move higher, higher, until you have attained the perfect perspective, the better perspective. Move higher still and look. Look down. Can you see it? Can you see the automobile? Follow the spray of light. It's moving eastward, through the mountains. It moves swiftly, quietly.

From above, to an eye overhead watching — your eye, our eye — the automobile cuts deftly through the night and through the storm. From above, from up here, there is no panting dog, there are no slapping windshield wipers, no quickened human heartbeats. There is only the hazy yellow light moving forward through the clouds and steam and water, and the solo auto — just a flashlight advancing, a flashlight following its light, following its high beams east along an otherwise blackened highway — looks almost peaceful. There are no towns lit up in the distance, no headlights from oncoming traffic, no streetlamps delineating the thin road's turns and dips.

But the sky? Where we are? So far up, the sky is a port-wine stain of brooding purple, punctuated by flame-like lightning, train-sized thunder. Several thousand feet higher, a place even higher than where we are now, a place from where we couldn't see the car, where we couldn't see anything, not even the rippling purple currents — several thousand feet higher, there are sheets of ice falling fast and loud, planks of snow like wood being battered and bullied by the atmosphere: a cacophony of ripping and tearing, a punching and hollering of ice pushing back against the steamy earth air, which shoots up fast and hot. Where the ice meets the heat, the sheets turn warm; they thin and loosen first like glass breaking and then like glass melting until the ice is water and the water is landing in waves — landing on the countryside, on the highway, on the roof of the isolated automobile so far beneath us.

But back to the car, the perspective is closer, tighter. The air-conditioning inches in humid and funky, a loamy mixture of wet soil and soft asphalt. The car — a tiny capsule of dryness — pushes forward awkwardly, hesitantly, with none of the finesse and speed suggested from above. There are no sounds from the radio, and perhaps no sounds either of any particular heartbeat, but the rain lands hard on the roof and the windshield wipers hit their marks with a troubling rhythm and the dog sits wide-eyed and panting, an uninterrupted string of drool extending from his gum to his shoulder. From the car, there is no sense of the bruise-y purple majesty battling in the ether overhead. From the car — the headlights its only guide — there are just the few dozen radiant feet of constantly moving rain and fog and road. Nothing more.

16

"What does that mean?" Maggie was leaning forward in the passenger seat. She was peering up at a road sign passing overhead.

"What?"

"That sign." Maggie pointed.

"Which sign?"

She pointed again.

"Are you pointing?" said Mark. "If you're pointing, I can't see what you're pointing at. I can't take my eyes off the road."

The windshield wipers were once again on full speed.

"You're right," said Maggie. "You're right. I'm sorry." She turned in her seat as they passed beneath the sign, as if turning might bring it back into view. But all she could see through the rear window was a glassy blackness. She wished Mark had been the one to notice the sign.

"Be specific," said Mark. "It's fine. Just tell me what it said."

"It doesn't matter," said Maggie. But it did matter. Of course it mattered.

Mark pressed the brakes and the car slowed even more. They

were going — max — twenty-five miles an hour now, but even this felt too fast.

"What did it say, Maggie? Please."

"It's just —" Maggie looked down at the map on her phone.

"Is this our exit or isn't it?" Mark said.

She wanted to use her forefinger and thumb to zoom in on the tiny graphic, but she was afraid she'd lose the original image.

Mark said her name again. "Is it or isn't it? Do I turn or not?" His voice was quick, which left her flustered.

"It's just —" Maggie slapped at her forehead twice, like a child jockeying forth the words. It was a gesture she knew Mark hated, but she couldn't help herself just then. "Yes." She spat out the word, slapping herself one more time. "This is our exit, or it should be, but what does it mean that there's no reentry? What does it mean that it's a northbound exit with no reentry?"

"Jesus," said Mark. "Did it say that? Is that what the sign said?" The exit was only a few hundred yards in front of them now.

"I didn't see any sign that said that. Are you sure you did?"

Of course he hadn't seen the sign. The highway was black. There were no streetlights and the sign wasn't illuminated. It had been a fluke — a ridiculous combination of quality headlights and serendipitous timing — that Maggie had seen it at all.

"Yes," she said. "I'm sure."

"Should I pull over?"

"I don't know," said Maggie. She felt like a teenager. She felt she shouldn't be the one answering a question like that; felt he shouldn't have been asking in the first place. Why couldn't Mark show some confidence for once, some real wherewithal? It was draining sometimes, being always expected to be an equal in everything. She longed to be taken care of.

"I'll pull over," he said. "That makes the most sense." But he didn't sound convinced.

Mark steered the car to the right shoulder, the rear tires skidding, and came to a rough stop. To the left was the empty dark highway. To the right was a veritable rain forest filled with unknowns and unsavories. The sound of the hail was nearly deafening now.

Maggie turned again to look out the rear window. "Is this safe?" she said. "This can't be safe."

It was true they hadn't seen another car since the hail had started, but all it would take was one truck, one semi with a driver asleep at the wheel, and they'd be a crumpled box of sardines.

"Let me see your phone," said Mark.

She handed it to him.

"Where are we?"

She pointed.

"Here?"

"There."

Mark held the phone closer to his face.

"I can't see anything," he said. "Can't you zoom in?"

"I'll lose the original image," she said. "Or I might and then what?"

Gerome, who had been sitting, now stood and took a step forward toward the front seat. Maggie scratched beneath his chin. "It's okay, boy," she said. "You're a good monkey."

Drool hit the center console.

Mark said, "Can you do something about him? Please? I'm trying to make sense of all this."

"He's scared," Maggie said. "The rain is so loud. He doesn't know why we're stopped."

"Jesus —" Mark put an elbow into Gerome's chest and manhandled him into the backseat. "Just — Just get back. Sit down. Yes, sit. Sit. You know the word. That's right. Good boy. Good monkey. Shh. Yes. Now just — Yes. Good boy. Stay there. Good."

Once the dog was repositioned and calmed, Mark turned to Maggie. He let out a deep breath and then switched on the overhead light. "What did the sign say exactly? Close your eyes. Tell me exactly."

Maggie switched the light off. Mark turned it on again. Maggie switched it off and — against her better judgment — let slip, "But they'll see."

Mark cocked his head. Even in the darkness, she saw him do it — the same slow deliberate cock as whenever he caught her at something less than ideal: canceling an appointment, overcooking a steak, walking the dog in her robe.

"What do you mean: *They'll see?* What do you mean by that?"

Maggie shook her head. "I didn't say that."

"You did."

"I didn't mean anything by it."

"But you did, Maggie. You meant something."

Maggie shook her head more aggressively. She was desperate to get going again. She was desperate for Mark to put the car in gear and take the exit — reentry or no — and get them to a hotel. A safe, dry, quiet hotel with doors that locked and windows that closed and (*oh god*) what she wouldn't give just to have time speed up! She would trade anything for the sun suddenly to rise, for the darkness to immediately give way, for the rain simply to stop. As easy as changing a channel. Just let it be tomorrow already. *I'll give anything,* she thought. *A baby. A firstborn baby. Anything. I'll make a deal with the devil. You name it; I'll give it.*

From the backseat, Gerome let out a moan, half whistle, half sigh. He too was anxious for tomorrow.

"I just meant . . ." Maggie sought to explain, but she couldn't. To clarify — to correctly elucidate what she'd meant — she would have to go too far back. She would need to begin with childhood and imagination and the way, on occasion, she had indulged in letting her mind wander: the thought of a minor break-in turned a hideously bloody event; the notion of a car crash that saved a squirrel but left her family lifeless and limbless only blocks from their home; the idea of a kidnapping in which she, Maggie, was tortured, abused for years. She would have to explain how the fantasies had made her feel. But in order to do that, she'd have to find a way of expressing the disturbing chemistry of fear and attraction. She'd have to admit that the fantasies which led to the fear — or the fear which led to the fantasies; she didn't know; she was stymied even now! — she'd have to concede they felt *good*. She had liked, as a child, the way her heartbeat would quicken and her body's temperature would rise and fall abruptly, a dizziness akin to fainting. She had liked the night sweats and the way her skin felt sticky between her T-shirt and stomach. She'd enjoyed all of it, every bit of it, and she couldn't as a child shut a fantasy down until she'd let it reach its natural, most punishing resolution — a sort of orgasm, though she'd never have been able to describe it as such back then. But she couldn't shut it down until she'd pushed it so far that she was sure — quite sure, quite deliciously and deliriously positive — that no one in the world had ever imagined her particular fantasy before.

She thought she'd gotten past all this; she thought she'd grown out of it, away from it. She'd gone to college, to vet school, gotten married, opened her own clinic. She'd become an adult, given up her fantasies. She felt a true participant of the world. She enjoyed her interactions with other people. But there'd been that night in the alley — *Lady. Lady.* — and her sense of security had fluttered, a receipt resting unguarded on a windowsill. She'd done as she was told: she went to a therapist, took a Valium here and there, meditated most mornings, and then, just as she'd sensed herself recuperating, returning to the woman she'd miraculously grown into, those detectives had shown up with photos of the coed, and any sense of renewed security had finally flitted off, the receipt picked up gingerly on a breeze and carried effortlessly away, at first within reach, but then out, then gone. The lurid fantasies had returned overnight — the fantasies and the night sweats.

Saying this to Mark — saying it to anyone, really, including her therapist — was madness, sheer madness. She couldn't stomach the thought of being regarded as some nineteenth-century parlor maid who claimed ghosts in the pantry. The thought of being dismissed, of being dismissible at all, made Maggie quiver with anger.

Of course, she might have tried to laugh away her morbid adolescent fantasies — *Ha! Ha! Ha!* — to laugh away her habit as a childhood peculiarity, but Mark would have seen through the effort — *heard* through the effort — and so she knew not to try.

Oh, snap out of it!

She reached up and switched on the overhead. Mark's expression was soft, tender. Not an ounce of the displeasure she'd been so quick to assume.

"I was being hysterical." She was matter-of-fact. "I don't know what else to say."

She gestured toward the overhead lights and shrugged. "No one can see us because no one is around," she said. "I'm not crazy. I'm just wound up."

Mark put a hand to her cheek. *Good husband. Best husband.* He stroked her skin with his thumb. "You scare me sometimes," he said.

The sky was a garbage truck of sound, the hotel still another twenty miles from the exit — once they finally took it, *if* they finally took it — and sunrise still so many hours away. Yet Mark was scared of Maggie? It was enough to make her laugh. Though of course she knew better. *Of course I know better.*

"Is this our exit?" he said at last. "Is that what you think?"

Maggie nodded. He took his hand away from her cheek. She trembled in her seat.

"Then it doesn't matter that there's no reentry." He flipped off the overhead. "All it means is that tomorrow we have to take different back roads out of here. Instead of spitting us out where we are now — Wait. Here. I'll show you." Mark turned on Maggie's phone. A tiny spray of light hit his chin so that his nose cast a funny shadow across his lips, almost as if he had no mouth at all.

"See this baby road up here?" Mark said.

Maggie wasn't looking at the screen. It didn't matter anymore.

"Right here," he said. "This is where we'll reenter the freeway, and it looks like we'll make some progress when we do it. It looks like we'll ultimately come out ahead."

17

The road was narrow. Mark was still driving. Once they had taken the exit and the turn off the exit and then the turn off the turn off the exit, they'd started a slow ascent into the mountains. The road they were on now was more slender than the last. There was so much tree cover that the rain seemed almost to have lightened. Or maybe it actually had lightened. Maybe the second storm was finally passing. Or was it the third? The branches — thick with wet lush leaves — were low, lower than they should have been because of the water weighing them down.

There were limbs in the road. Limbs, leaves, debris, beer cans. Mark knew Maggie would be concentrating on the beer cans. There were no houses, no signs of life, but there were beer cans. He knew what she was capable of doing with that sort of evidence — hunters up to no good, terrorists hiding in the hills, kidnappers building their next torture bunker. Maybe she'd always been this way. Maybe he'd overlooked it, which would make it his fault in a sense. Perhaps she hadn't changed at all. Perhaps he'd finally started paying attention. It made him sad for them both.

When he was a boy, Mark would sometimes find himself filled up with indignation, with what he'd call now an animal sort of fury. It came from nothing, out of nowhere. He'd be walking in the woods, kicking sticks or jumping on twigs, and he'd suddenly feel a hot rush come over his entire body, like a blanket soaked in boiling water then wrapped abruptly and tightly around him. He'd throw himself to the ground when he felt it, fists and feet pummeling the dirt, tearing apart the leaves, terrifying the branches. Anything he could touch he destroyed.

Later, a teenager, when he finally discovered Wordsworth, Emerson, Thoreau — those men who understood isolation and what it was not just to be alive, but to be human, to be a man and in nature — he diagnosed those early fits of fury as the Grown Man Inside, the Man Already a Man, trapped in the small boy's body. When, as a teenager, the temper returned — as it often did, though he'd many years earlier learned to stop throwing himself to the ground — he began to visualize this man who was inside, the man responsible for the wrath. He found that the image calmed him. He further discovered that he could control the image — not necessarily the man — but if he closed his eyes and concentrated hard enough, he could take the picture of this man (this future iteration of himself, fully realized) and make him move. He could, for instance, will the man to jump up and down, punch the air, punch the earth, fling himself to the ground in Mark's stead.

He considered the man his grown-up twin, dressed always in whatever flannel or sweatshirt Mark happened to be wearing on a particular day. Back then, he'd taken the man very seriously. On the one hand, he fully understood him to be a figment of his own imagination. On the other, he believed the man to be a very real indication of what he — Mark — was destined one day to become. He believed that he had walked through one of those hidden doorways in the brain that only the very special ever entered.

122

Not only had he found the door, but he'd opened it and gone inside and met himself. It was a part of the brain that only geniuses and outliers accessed. This was something Mark believed absolutely as a teenager.

Now, as an adult, he wasn't sure what he believed. He knew to laugh at the idea of an imaginary adult version of himself dressed identically to his teenage self (the flannel shirt, the baggy khakis). At the same time, the man — now more a shadowy outline — still came in useful with his adult fits of anger. From time to time, when necessary, he was still able to close his eyes, conjure the figure, and have it lasso all the ire swirling about in the blackness of his mind. Just now, for instance, weepy willowy Maggie at his side, Mark was imagining the shadowy outline: arms above his head, legs planted squarely in the terra firma of Mark's brain matter, mouth wide open and screaming for his life.

It struck him that Maggie was saying his name, perhaps had been saying his name for quite some time.

"Are you paying attention?" she asked. "Mark? Are you paying attention?"

Without realizing, Mark had brought the car to a halt at the world's smallest, darkest intersection. The road they were on had come to an abrupt end. In front of them was dense dark forest and in front of that a tiny green sign — illuminated now by their headlights — with one arrow to the right and one arrow to left. There were no route numbers, no road names. Just two arrows — right or left — in case you couldn't see that straight ahead was nothing but trees and brush and early summer overgrowth.

"Are you paying attention?" she said again. "Do you want me to drive?"

As if Maggie would trade places with him.

As if she'd get out of the car and shuffle her way around to the driver's side at this time of night.

As if.

"I'm waiting for you to direct me," he said.

Maggie didn't say anything. She was looking at her lap now, looking at her tiny glowing screen. He cracked his knuckles. All these people all the time shining a light at their faces, voluntarily giving into the machine, voluntarily zapping their own brain cells. He could practically see his wife getting dumber. Right now. At this exact second, he could picture the brain cells being zapped by the ambient blue light. Jesus, and she hadn't even been raised on the Internet. She'd been raised on books, on paper and pens just as he had. But she'd succumbed. Somewhere along the line — before the mugging, after the mugging, did it matter? — she'd succumbed to the media, to the devices, to the wires and webs and whole wide world of Internet make-believe.

It wasn't just his students. It was his wife, too. It was everything and everyone. The world was ruled by technology; disturbed by nature.

What happened to real maps? That's what Mark wanted to know. What happened to good old-fashioned red and orange and blue and yellow maps that you could hold in your hands, rub between your thumb and index finger — maps that could be folded and jostled and looked at whenever you goddamned pleased and not just when the gods of cell service deemed it appropriate or convenient?

He closed his eyes. The little man punched the air as hard as he could — once, twice, three times — then retreated into the shaded obscurity of his brain.

"Right or left?" Mark said.

"I think," Maggie said, then stopped short. "I mean, I think right. Take a right. It's what the map says. Unless there's another road a little farther."

"Farther where, Maggie? There's a forest in front of us."

"It's just ..." she said. He was making her nervous, which meant it would take her twice as long before she would make sense. "It's just the map doesn't indicate a turn — one way or the other."

"What do you mean?"

"I mean this dead end doesn't exist."

"Of course it exists. I'm looking at it."

"But on the map," she said. "It doesn't exist." She gestured to her phone.

Okay. Okay, so here. This. This right here. This — *this* was what Mark was talking about. Right here. Right now. Mark and Maggie were in a car on a road that had clearly come to an end. He was looking at it. He could see with his own two eyes that the dead end existed. But Maggie was looking at a phone. She was telling him that what he could see — what they could *both* technically see because neither of them was blind — didn't exist because it wasn't on her phone. What it was, at the end of the day — what it really, possibly was — was that Maggie was killing him.

He took a deep breath.

"From where we are now, is the hotel north, south, east, what?"

"Take a right," she said.

"How do you know? If this turn doesn't exist, then how do you know?"

"Because the hotel is to the right of here."

He held his hand out. "Show me," he said.

She clutched the phone to her chest.

"Show me."

"No."

"Just show me where we are."

"No."

"Are you fucking with me, Maggie? Are you goading me? Because it's working. It really is. Just show me where we are."

She unclenched the phone but didn't hand it to him. Instead, she cradled it like a miniature baby in her palm. "We don't show up on the phone anymore," she said at last. "So I'm having to wing it."

"Wing it?"

These were the facts, as Mark saw them: It was past two in the morning. They were on some microscopic back road in West Virginia. Mark could barely see shit. The wipers weren't working worth a fuck. Mangled leaves were glommed up and down the sides of both blades. The windshield would be scratched to hell by morning. And Maggie, dry and safe and cozy, was over there in the passenger seat with her personal bullshit device *winging* it?

"This is it," she said. "This is the turn. Take a right. I'm sure."

Fine, he thought. *Fuck it.*

Mark put the car in gear and, the headlights their only guide, took the turn.

What, after all, was the worst that could happen?

18

The rain stopped — Maggie was thankful for that at least — but the front windshield was starting to fog up, and so now Mark rolled down the driver's-side window. They were going maybe twenty miles an hour.

"What are you doing?" said Maggie.

Gerome lifted his head, sniffed, then went back to sleep. He was too tired to bother with anything anymore. If only Maggie could feel fatigue like that, all her problems would be solved.

"I'm getting some fresh air. It's too close in here."

When Mark proposed, some eight years earlier, they'd been lying together on the couch in their first apartment in Georgetown. Mark had just finished his dissertation; Maggie would earn her DVM in the spring. It was winter and dark out. At midnight, when the snow started, they opened all the windows and climbed under a blanket in the living room. It was so cold they could see their breath, but they wanted to watch the snow fall and they wanted to inhale that crisp snowy air and the smells of the wood fires from the row houses down the way. Mark's manner was twitchy and, after only a few minutes, he said it was too close where they were huddled together under the blanket. He'd gotten off the couch abruptly and disappeared into the bedroom. For a moment Maggie feared he'd lost interest in her. When he reappeared several minutes later, a small velvet box in his hands, she understood. Her fears disappeared completely. She wondered now if he ever thought about that night or if it was a memory she alone kept alive.

"Why does it matter that I've got a window down?" said Mark. Maggie stared out the front windshield.

"Gerome isn't bothered. So what's your problem?"

"Never mind," said Maggie. "I don't even care." She knew — really, truly she did — that it was silly to be scared of an open window. If they were vulnerable, they were vulnerable. And if they were safe, they were safe. One window up or down wouldn't change anything.

"I know what it is," said Mark. He was cranky, a sign of exhaustion. "Yep. I know what it is." He knocked on the steering wheel with an open hand as though he'd come to some unforeseen and therefore grand realization. Maggie sighed.

"It's nothing," she said. "I'm tired. That's all. It's humid with the window down. But I don't care. Really."

"You know what your problem is?" Mark said.

To be asleep, to be blissfully lifted away from this moment, this night, that's all Maggie wanted.

"Your problem is that you think the boogeyman is lurking," he said.

She rubbed at her neck, at the place where that hideous bruise had been. She closed her eyes, and there was the coed, prostrate, her chin angled to that ill-fated degree, her wet hair pressed against the base of the toilet. Was it wet from the struggle? Or had she been showering when the man found her? At so many times of the day, we expose ourselves to chance.

"And do you know what your problem is?" she asked at last.

"My problem?" Mark snorted. "I'd love to know. Yes. Fire away. Let's hear it."

"You pretend it doesn't exist."

"That what doesn't exist?"

"Evil."

Mark snorted again, and Maggie felt suddenly sorry for him. This man, this husband of hers, was completely unaware of the complexities of the human brain. She felt sorry for all men, really — for all those penises just getting in the way of real insight. They lacked imagination; they believed only what they already knew.

Mark picked up his speed, though the road was no less narrow or unfamiliar than before. Maggie grabbed the inside handle of the passenger side door. She did it for effect, but — if Mark even noticed — the gesture had an opposite outcome than the one she desired. He sped up.

"You're going too fast," she said. She gripped the door more tightly.

As they rounded the next turn, an inside corner that hugged the mountain's increasing height, Mark drifted across the yellow line.

"You're not paying attention," she said.

"I'm fine."

"Just slow down."

"There's no one else around." He picked up his speed even more, and a branch overhead, thick with wet green leaves, fell onto the hood of the car, then whipped against the windshield. Their vision was momentarily obscured.

Maggie put a hand on the dashboard as if to steady the entire car.

Mark hit the brakes and the branch flew away.

He pressed the gas again, now clutching at the steering wheel and leaning more forward in his seat.

As they rounded an outside corner, Maggie looked out and down, one hand still on the dashboard, the other holding on to the door. To her right, the edge of the mountain seemed to plunge itself into a steep cosmic darkness. She closed her eyes.

At Foster Beach last winter, a woman — alone, late at night — had driven her sedan off the seawall, plunging ten feet before cracking the ice and sinking into the subzero water. In the car, when the divers, many hours later, were able to salvage what was left, they found the woman's body of course. But in the trunk they also discovered two Mason jars, each filled with the fetus of a baby and a single plastic rose. Maggie had tried to imagine the life of the person, the woman, who might have placed her own babies in those Mason jars before driving off the seawall. What desperation that woman must have felt. What unmatched and severe loneliness and isolation.

"Please," Maggie said. She touched Mark's arm. "It's not safe. Just slow down."

"True fact," he said. There was something diabolic to the way his right cheek was positioned on his face. "Did you know that when the weatherman says there's a twenty percent chance of rain, he doesn't mean there's an eighty percent chance it won't? He means twenty percent of a specified region will absolutely feel rainfall. Did you know that? There's no chance to it at all except which area it will be."

Maggie wanted to slap him. If he hadn't been driving, it's possible she might very well have done it. He opened his mouth to say more, but just as he did — just as he licked his lips, took a breath in, and opened his mouth — a bright light appeared suddenly behind them.

"Fuck," Mark said. He flipped the rearview mirror so the light was out of his eyes. "Where the fuck did that come from?"

Maggie turned in her seat. Behind them — barreling toward them at great speed — was a large truck. There was a row of lights above the windshield, another on each of the side-view mirrors, and two more closer together just above the bumper. It looked like the face of a large black spider rapidly encroaching. Back on the highway, Maggie would have paid money for the camaraderie of another car. But here, where they were, for all intents and purposes essentially lost, the last thing she wanted was company.

"Who does that?" Maggie said. "Why are they so close to us?"

Mark looked into the rearview, then raised his hand to shield his eyes or maybe to get a better view. "Are those hunting lights?"

"Stunning deer," she said. "It makes me sick."

"Do they want to go around?" he said. "I can't tell. I can't just pull over." He was still shielding his eyes from the light.

The truck swerved into the other lane, as if to pass, but then swerved back behind them.

"Are they drunk?" Mark asked.

"This doesn't feel right," she said. "Did you just speed up?" She turned forward in her seat and again clutched at the door.

They drove on, the truck no fewer than twenty feet behind them.

"I don't like this," she said.

"He's not giving me a choice," he said. "He's right on my ass."

There was no place to turn, no strip of grass to pull onto. There was simply the mountain wall to the left, the mountain edge to the right and, between, the meager two-lane blacktop.

The truck flashed its lights.

"If I slow down," Mark said, "he'll ram right into us."

Maggie bit at her lips. What kind of people would be out on

a night like this, at an hour like this, after a storm like the one they'd driven through? What kind of people — other than Mark and Maggie, who were stranded, displaced, without other options — would voluntarily be out on the road rather than home tucked in bed? There was only one answer to that question: people who were up to no good. Perhaps it was one of their bumper stickers — idiotic, liberal bumper stickers: PRO-CHOICE, NEUTER/SPAY, YES WE CAN. In a place like this, their car practically shouted, *I am other. I am other. I am other.* She could have kicked herself for applying those stickers to begin with. Why did a person need to advertise her views every single place she went?

"Oh god. Oh god," she said.

From behind, another brighter beam now appeared, not from an additional car but from atop the row of lights above the truck's windshield — a sort of high-intensity spotlight.

"Mark!" said Maggie. She covered her eyes. The light was blinding. "Can you see?"

"How much farther?" said Mark. "Do you think we're close?"

Maggie hunched over in her seat in order to block as much of the glare as possible. There were black circles in her vision, as when a child she once ventured a forbidden glance at the sun during an eclipse. She cupped a hand over her phone and looked down. The screen was darker now. It wasn't just her vision. The battery was dying.

"If we're where I think we are, then it should be —" The screen darkened more; she could barely see the map. She sat up slightly and looked out the window. Like a gift, like a tiny little present forgotten during a Christmas celebration but remembered as the tree is being dismantled and the ornaments put away, there was a sign on Maggie's side of the road. She had looked up and out at just the right moment, and the headlights

of their car — or, who knows? Maybe it was the truck's search-
light behind them — had shone brightly and squarely upon it.

"There!" Maggie said. She pointed and her finger hit the window. "I saw it," she said. "I saw the sign. Holidays Inn. It's just
ahead." She was dizzy with relief, giddy with excitement. She'd
seen the sign. She'd seen it!

The truck behind them revved its engine. Maggie, her heartbeat racing, her eyes strained small and tight, turned in her seat
to look, but the headlights veered suddenly to the right. She
watched as the lights moved eastward and down, down, down
into the woodland until its beams were too small to register or
the trees too dense to reveal.

It was quiet and dark, and they were again alone.

Mark massaged his eyes. "Jesus," he said. "I thought I'd go
blind. Which way now?"

"Was there even a road back there?" said Maggie, still staring
into the blackness behind them. "I didn't see a road back there."

"Who cares?" said Mark. "Just tell me where to go now."

"Straight for half a mile," she said. "That's what the sign said."

She turned forward in her seat, her hand mechanically covering her heart. She waited.

Sure enough, in less than half a mile, the tree cover broke, and
they found themselves at last at a four-way intersection. The traffic light overhead was out, but it was a real-live intersection with
a real-live traffic light.

Maggie let out a deep breath.

The sky overhead — mercifully without rain — was a deep
shiny purple. To the left was a dark two-story building and a
small parking lot. To the right was a series of smaller dark buildings. Straight ahead, the road appeared to dead end into a cul-
de-sac. There were no lights anywhere, just the limited luminos-

ity of the cloud-covered moon. They were on top of a mountain, one that had been shaved bald and poured with concrete.

"So where's the hotel?" Mark said.

Maggie looked down at her phone. The screen flickered, then went black. "It's dead," she said.

"But the sign said half a mile? Straight ahead?"

"I'm sure of it," said Maggie, and she was.

"Maybe it's a little farther."

"Maybe," she said.

Mark drove slowly through the intersection. Rain puddles — *pshhh pshhh pshhh* — splashed gracefully under their tires. But what Maggie had guessed was right: it was just a large cul-de-sac on the other side.

"Is this a power plant?" Mark said. He parked the car halfway around the circle. The headlights shone onto a chain-link fence. Behind the fence was yet another building, this one low and long and also dark. "I think it's some kind of power plant," he said.

"Just keep going," she said. "Go around the circle one more time. But go slowly so I can get a look at all these buildings."

Mark put the car in gear and started to creep in the direction of the intersection.

"Oh my god," she said.

"What?"

Maggie couldn't believe it. It was so obvious.

"What?"

"That," she said. She pointed at the two-story building. "That's the hotel."

Mark shook his head. "No," he said. "It's dark."

"Exactly," she said. How had it taken her so long to put it all together? "There's no power."

"But all the hotels have power."

"All the *other* hotels have *generators*."

"But Gwen made a reservation," said Mark. "You said so."

Poor Mark. He wasn't catching on. But to Maggie, it made terrific and immediate sense. She nearly wanted to laugh. Gwen had made them a reservation *online*, at the only hotel with a vacancy. And it was the only hotel with a vacancy because the website wasn't communicating with the hotel. Because the hotel didn't have power. Of course. And when Gwen tried calling, no one had answered. The phone lines were probably down too. Of course, of course. Oh, what idiots they'd all been!

"Pull in," said Maggie. "Let's see what the deal is."

"But we can't stay here."

"Just pull in and let me see."

Mark inched the car into the parking lot. There were ten or so cars parked side by side. He pulled up to the entrance, which was lit up by a few paper bags with tea candles inside them. How had Maggie not noticed these when they'd driven by the first time?

She opened the passenger door. The air felt swampy. "Just wait here, okay?"

"But if they don't have power, then they don't have —"

She didn't bother letting him finish. She was ready to be out of the car, ready to be stationary for a few hours. She needed to lie down and sleep safely behind a locked door. Her body demanded a break from the world. It was nearly four in the morning. Did it matter that there wasn't power? Not for a minute.

Inside, the lobby was muggy, humid — *close*, thought Maggie — and the front desk was lined with more tea candles. The room had a homey glimmer about it, but there was no one actually manning the desk.

Maggie stepped closer; her armpits were damp. She was aware of a slight funk drifting up from her shirt. Somewhere behind the desk, in a back room, there was music playing, something soothing and familiar. She couldn't quite put her finger on it. She stepped closer still and saw that, on the counter, there was a little silver bell on top of a small sliver of paper. *Ring me*, it said.

Hesitantly, Maggie held out her hand. She'd seen little bells like this before, but she'd never actually had to ring one. They'd never been on the road this late, and there'd never been a time when any lobby had been totally deserted.

She was nervous, but she was also determined. She believed she was mere moments away from lying in a bed, mere moments away from sleep.

She brushed the bell once with her ring finger.

"You don't need to do that," a woman's voice said.

Maggie jumped a little.

"I'm right here," the voice said.

Maggie looked around, but still she didn't see anyone.

"I see you," it said. "Just give me one second, please."

The voice was coming, Maggie realized, from some place low behind the front desk. She leaned over to look.

There, sitting cross-legged on the floor, was a very small woman. Her arms, from wrist to elbow, were lit up with glowing plastic bracelets. Around her neck was a clunky glowing necklace. She appeared to be going through the open cabinet in front of her.

Maggie retreated to her own side of the counter. "Sure," Maggie said. "Take your time."

The song from the back room was an instrumental version of something that Maggie usually associated with lyrics. What was it? It was organ-heavy, maybe even a bit ritzy, out of place for a secluded hotel in West Virginia. Was it "Spanish Harlem"? Was she making that up? It sounded like "Spanish Harlem," or at least a version she'd once heard at the Green Mill back in Chicago. She turned her head to the side and angled her ear toward the music. She listened.

It was another minute before the woman on the other side

of the counter finally stood, during which time Maggie was able to see that the lobby — which she'd already gauged as quite large — was even larger than she'd first understood. And now, Maggie's eyes adjusting, she began to make out little glow sticks, similar to the ones the woman was wearing, tied, for light, to various lamps and fixtures all around the room. In the planter at the entrance, she now saw, someone had stuck several dozen of them decoratively around a fern.

"You got to replace them every hour is the thing."

Maggie jumped again, but only slightly.

Even standing, the woman was not much taller than the counter. She gestured toward the fern. "Pretty much I finish getting them lit up and they lose their light and I have to do it all over again. Passes the time, though."

"The glow sticks?" asked Maggie.

"We been like this for three days."

"Like this?"

"No power."

"For three days?" said Maggie. They'd only heard about the storms that afternoon.

"Tornado number one took out the power lines and the phone lines. We were first in line for help, but then the real cities got hit by the second storm and, you know, they're cities, so our dumb-fuck governor redirected the assistance. More people equals more need." The woman held up a small neon bag. "You know how they work?"

Maggie shook her head.

The woman tore open the bag and pulled out three dim sticks. She handed one to Maggie. "Bend that till it clicks."

Maggie looked down at the little piece of plastic in her hand. "Like this?" she asked.

"Yep, but keep going until —" The glow stick clicked and came instantly to life in Maggie's hands. "And voilà," said the woman. "You're a natural."

Maggie smiled.

"You here for a room?" the woman said.

Maggie explained that she was traveling with her husband and their dog, that her mother-in-law had made a reservation online, that the website had indicated a vacancy, and that they'd in fact already paid.

During Maggie's short speech, the woman nodded, every once in a while glancing in the direction of the back room.

"So here's the deal," she said when Maggie was finished. "We got rooms. We got clean towels and clean sheets and cold running water. We got glow sticks. But that's all we got. We do not have air-conditioning. We do not have hot water. Repeat: No air-conditioning. No hot water."

Maggie started to speak, but the woman stopped her.

"And with regard to payment, you'll have to let me take a carbon of your credit card. When we get our power back, we'll weed through the online payments and the in-person payments. But I can't give you a room without the carbon."

Maggie knew the air-conditioning was going to be a problem for Mark, but she also knew he was too tired to keep driving. They both were. He wouldn't like this business of the credit card — and practically he would have been right not to — but she could get it taken care of now, before he came in, and he'd never have to know about it.

"What about our dog?" said Maggie. "You're okay with a dog?"

"The more the merrier," said the woman.

"Then we have a deal," said Maggie. "I'd like a room."

19

Mark flipped off the headlights, rolled down the windows, and killed the engine. It was hot out, but the fresh air felt good in his nostrils. He left the key in the ignition so he could listen to the radio. There was a feeling in his gut not of childhood, but of that beautiful purgatory between childhood and adulthood. Yes, with the windows rolled down and with the sudden solitude — sharp solitude there in that car on the top of a tiny mountain town miles and miles from anywhere legit — and with the magenta darkness all around him, he remembered keenly what he'd felt so long ago first as a teenager and then as a young man just starting out in the world. He remembered the feeling of life, how big it was, how conquerable the world seemed then. Behind him: boyhood antics. In front of him: glory, love, sex, fame, ambition, life, anything he wanted. Yes, just now, just at this very moment, he remembered it all so vividly. What he needed was a Springsteen song. Something gritty. Something as full of vim and vigor as he'd been so long ago.

He kept the volume low as he flipped through the stations. The first three were nothing but static. The fourth was talk radio.

He knew it was evangelical from the extra vibrato in the man's voice. It was only a minute before he grew restless with its content. *If man came from apes, then how come apes still exist? etc., etc.* — to which Mark would have retorted, applying their slant logic: If Eve came from Adam, why do men still exist? But it wasn't as entertaining without Maggie there listening too, which obviously said something awfully small and petty about him — that he couldn't enjoy it without Maggie there *not* enjoying it. He knew it. And he was sorry. He really was. But he also knew it meant something loving and solid about the two of them. She drove him crazy, but that's how he knew he still cared. They really were like a country song, which he would have settled for if he couldn't find Springsteen — Johnny, Waylon, Merle, maybe a little Willie.

The thing was Mark needed her around, no matter how batty she got. She was still Maggie, his Maggie. Christ, he needed to lay off her every once in a while. He needed to temper his expectations because — Yes! Expectations! Wasn't that absolutely part of the problem? Wasn't he always expecting just a little too much from everyone, but from Maggie especially? He was. He was.

The only other channel was news. It came in staticky, but Mark didn't mind. He leaned back in his seat, shut his eyes, and listened. The weather had top billing. There were outages from Indiana straight through to western Virginia. His parents had been right. Just a few hours earlier, the president had declared federal emergencies in four states. Congress was in a brand-new uproar. Money was on everyone's minds.

The next story up was out of California. A university had issued a statement: it was mere weeks away from unveiling its development of full artificial intelligence. After the statement, the anchor read aloud from an old interview with Stephen Hawking. "... could spell the end of the human race." Mark reclined his seat as far as it would go. The end of the human race ... The idea itself — the end of humanity — didn't trouble him necessarily, but that humans would be responsible bothered him to no end. He remembered when Hawking had given that interview a couple years back, and he remembered the jeering that had gone on in the department in the days following. Most of his colleagues resisted the idea of an intelligence that could surpass their own. Of course, most of his colleagues were narcissists. They resisted the notion that artificial intelligence would ever be able to redesign itself of its own volition, and so obviously they rejected the possibility that it would eventually supersede humanity. Perhaps they were only a few weeks from finding out.

In the backseat, Gerome yawned. Mark turned onto his side and scratched the dog's head.

"It's been a long day, hasn't it?" he said.

Gerome stood and stretched.

"You want a walk?"

The dog nosed forward and licked at Mark's ear.

"How about a walk, then?"

Mark patted the front seat, and Gerome climbed over the center console and took Maggie's spot. He sat bolt upright, like he expected to be buckled into place. Maggie hated it when Mark let the dog in front, but she loved it when Mark was tender.

"A fair trade," Mark said. "Good boy."

He started the car and pulled it into a proper parking spot, then he hooked Gerome's leash to his collar and the two got out on the driver's side together.

They were standing in the middle of what he guessed was maybe ten acres of cleared mountaintop development. There was the hotel and there was the plant across the street and there was some sort of office park across from that. But nothing more.

The forest resumed behind and down from the hotel. Mark couldn't see well enough to explore that far, and he didn't want to walk in what he imagined was thick wet grass and mud, so he opted to pace the perimeter of the parking lot, which was lined by a narrow strip of grass. Gerome peed instantly.

Tree frogs were chirping in the distance. It would be morning in only a few hours. Mark's head was killing him and his eyes were sore. If he hadn't had those beers, then he probably would've been good to drive straight through. As it was, he needed shut-eye. At the very least, he needed to lie supine for a while. Maggie was taking forever, which he assumed was a good sign. She was getting them a room, and any minute she'd come out and retrieve the two of them.

But she didn't come out, not immediately anyway. So after Gerome had peed a second time, the two of them went in.

Tropical was how he'd describe the air if anyone asked, which no one did, so he kept the word to himself. Maggie was standing at the hotel's front desk; she was blousing her shirt for air. There was a couple standing opposite her, a very small woman and a very large man. Maggie was laughing.

Mark approached.

"What's the deal?" he said. He didn't address the couple.

"We have a room," Maggie said. "And glow sticks." She held up two plastic baggies.

"I told her," said the small woman across from them, "we got cold running water and clean towels. We do not have air-conditioning. We do not have hot water."

"Are there fans?" said Mark.

"We got fans," said the large man. "We got plenty of fans. But we don't got power." He laughed as though what he'd said was quite funny. "We also got two fridges filled with spoiled food if you're interested."

"Isn't there a generator?"

"That broke two days ago," Maggie said.

Mark looked back and forth between his wife and the couple. If there weren't fans, then what on earth were they still doing there?

"This is Tina," said Maggie, "and this is Pete."

Pete held out his hand. Gerome jumped up and licked it. Mark yanked on the leash.

"Sorry," Mark said.

Pete wiped his hand on his pants. "Not a problem. We got seven at home. He can probably smell them on me."

"Dogs?"

"Pure breeds. Boxers. We got two puppies right now. Folks say they want to come by to look, but nobody comes by just to look. Once you've seen 'em, you want 'em. I don't even have to advertise. So we're real careful about who we let see 'em." Pete paused and looked at Tina. "Ain't we?" He nudged her.

Maggie took the leash from Mark. "Tina and Pete are engaged," she said to Mark. "Pete doesn't actually work here. He's just helping Tina while the power's off."

Pete held up his arms and flexed. He kissed his biceps one at a time, then smiled. "Call me the bodyguard."

"How nice," Mark said. He turned to Maggie. "If there's not air-conditioning, what's the point? We won't sleep. We won't even relax. Look at Gerome. He's already panting. He can barely breathe."

Maggie looked down at Gerome, who looked up at her and seemed to smile. She scratched under his chin. "Panting is your way of sweating," she said to the dog. "It's healthy."

"You two need a minute?" Tina asked.

"We don't need a minute," Maggie said. "It'll be fine." She handed Mark the glow sticks. "I need to lie down. So do you."

As if on cue, Gerome yawned.

"Bodyguard, eh?" Mark nodded. "There's a lot of crime up here? People up to no good?"

Maggie glowered at him. Mark knew the effect of his question, but he was irritated that she hadn't consulted him, pissed at the plan of paying money to sleep in a sealed-up room when they could just as easily sleep in the car with the engine running. He'd be much more comfortable in the front seat than in a room without air. Christ, he'd nearly drifted off while he was waiting for her! The car was plenty comfortable.

"No, no," said Tina. "It's real safe up here."

It was not what Mark was hoping for.

"But there's a certain type," she added.

Better, thought Mark.

"There's drugs on the other side of the mountain. Big trucks, loud music. Your basic ruffian, you know? But we never had a problem. No riffraff or horse thieves up here."

Pete clucked his tongue. "Not entirely true, Miss Tina," he said. "With the current situation as is, there have been some 'instances.'" He made quotations with his fingers.

"Instances?" Maggie said.

Bingo, thought Mark. Five more minutes and they'd be back on the road. He was sure of it. They could sleep at the first truck stop. He was good for at least another hour if he had to be. In fact, he was probably good to drive straight through. He'd been wrong about the beers; they'd worn off completely. He had just needed some air; needed to stretch his legs. His eyes felt fine now. Everything felt fine. Do a couple jumping jacks, maybe a few squats, and then be back on the road. More than doable.

"Just some kids roughing up lawns at night and such," said Tina. "Nothing to do with us or the hotel."

Maggie nodded. Her face was shiny with sweat. "Just kids?" she said.

"You'll be fine," said Pete. "That's why I'm here. Plus, I got some buddies staying in a couple of the rooms just in case."

Maggie was nodding still. "Just in case?"

"Yep," said Pete. He flexed his arms again and grinned.

Mark felt sure he'd won.

Maggie sighed. "Well," she said. She looked at Mark. "If Pete says it's safe, then I guess it's safe."

20

Pete walked in front, shining the way with a floodlight. Mark was next, followed by Tina. Maggie and Gerome took the rear.

Maggie was surprised when they were led into a stairwell. She'd assumed they'd get a room on the main level. She was further surprised when Pete walked them not up the stairs, but down. She hadn't realized — how could she have? — that the hotel was built into a hill and that there was an entire basement level with windows looking out onto a back parking lot.

What Maggie liked about Pete and Tina was their youthfulness, their hopefulness and straightforwardness. There was something pleasantly stupid about Pete in particular that Maggie found comforting, as if he lacked the imagination necessary to commit any wrong. It was the right way for a man to be if he didn't have imagination: sturdy and loyal as a dog. There seemed in him the quality of indefatigable goodness, something god-inspired, she suspected. And, sure, ordinarily she tended to fall on the more judgmental side of people who actually practiced religion, but right then she felt protected by its rote unwillingness to tolerate evil.

The nearness of the stairwell, the metallic *ping* of the steps beneath her shoes, brought on a memory, one she'd not entertained in ages. On the night they met, after Mark's confident approach aboard that riverboat, they'd found themselves not three minutes into their acquaintance in a steep enclosed stairwell between the second and first floors of the ship. If there was a light, it wasn't turned on. Maggie had led Mark, his hand in hers — though the way was no more familiar to her than to him — down and out and into the pink dusk of early evening. The intimacy of those few moments in that tight space nearly a decade ago — the swampy smell of the Potomac, the humidity seeping in from the water beneath them — came back to her now full force. That night — she'd never told Mark — but that night she'd been on the brink of agreeing to a proposed affair with her advisor, a married man nearing sixty. Thanks to Mark, to his singular attention, she'd never followed through on her intentions. Years later, after she and Mark were married, after they'd moved safely from DC to Chicago, she learned that her advisor had been bounced from the program. Videos had been discovered. There were dozens of young women, all students, and he'd secretly recorded his trysts with every one of them. If it hadn't been for Mark, Maggie might easily have been among those tapes. Her entire life might be something wholly different than what it was now. What she realized at this moment: her greatest fear — well, her greatest intellectual fear — was of being left behind emotionally. Of being the one caught in that terrible limbo of still being in love when the other person has already left the room.

Gerome was skittish on the steps. His pads kept slipping. If he were a smaller dog, Maggie would have picked him up.

At the bottom of the stairwell, Pete stopped, and so did the small crowd behind him. He raised the floodlight in front of a door.

"This is the rear exit," he said.

Mark nodded. "Got it."

"Normally you can't go out it, but the emergency alarm isn't on."

Mark nodded again. "Okay."

"So if you need to walk the dog, this is the easiest way out."

"Check," said Mark.

"Wait," said Maggie. "If the alarm isn't on, does that mean the door isn't locked?"

"We could bolt it," Tina said. "But that'd be against fire code."

Maggie didn't say anything. If Mark was waiting for a reaction, she wasn't going to give it to him.

Pete switched the aim of the floodlight. "Here's the door to the first-floor rooms." He held it open and the others filed past him. "Tina," he said, his voice suddenly soft. "Let's put them in 101." To Maggie, he said, "First door on the left there. You'll be nearby the exit. Good for the dog."

"Problem," said Tina, also now in a whisper.

Pete brushed by Maggie and Gerome; they were alone at the end of the hallway. Mark had his back to Maggie.

"What's up?" said Pete.

"101 wasn't closed," Tina said.

Pete used the floodlight to push the door open a little wider; from the hallway, he shined the light into the room. "It's empty," he said.

"Let's put them in another one anyway," said Tina. "I don't like that the door was open."

Maggie nudged Mark from behind. "Give me one of those glow sticks," she said. "I can't see what's going on."

"Better wait," said Tina. "They only last so long."

"Right," said Mark. "Good thinking." He put the glow sticks back in his pocket.

Pete led them down the hall to the next room. Maggie followed, still behind the pack. "This one's good," he said.

"Check it out for them," said Tina.

Pete opened the door and walked inside alone. After a few seconds he returned. "Clean," he said. "Empty."

"Go on in," said Tina. "Get your bearings before we take the light away."

Maggie and Gerome followed Mark in.

Pete shined the flashlight around the room. "Here's your bed," he said. "Here's your second bed. Extra pillows here. Bathroom here." He opened the bathroom door. "Your towels. The sink." At each item, he shined the light briefly, then moved on.

Maggie watched the various corners of the room light up and then darken. The images were fast and still, more like photographs than real life.

She thought of that terrible movie about forests and witchcraft and children standing in corners. She thought of the coed.

She'd made a mistake insisting on staying.

This wasn't a good idea at all.

"Pete," said Tina from the hallway, still whispering. "Show them about the glow sticks."

"Right," said Pete. He motioned for Maggie to join him in the bathroom. "If you tie one here"— with the flashlight, he lit up a small side mirror protruding from the wall —"then you get pretty good light and you don't need to waste more than one."

"Thanks," said Maggie. She was whispering too. "So there are other people on this floor?"

"There's a family across the way and some of my buddies down at the end. But you won't hear them."

"Where do you two sleep?"

"We're up in the office," he said.

"Oh," she said. "Right."

She wished she could sleep in the office with them. In numbers, there was safety.

She followed him from the bathroom back into the bedroom. Mark had snapped two of the glow sticks and was inspecting the windows.

Pete and Tina walked into the hallway.

"Be sure to lock the door behind us," said Tina.

Maggie nodded.

"You have to use the lever, though," Pete said. "It won't lock if you just close it."

"It won't?"

Tina took the floodlight and came back inside the room.

"See?" she said. She showed Maggie how the lever worked. "The regular locks are automated. Without power, they're a no-go."

"Oh," Maggie said. What else had she failed to consider? It was one thing to sleep without a/c; it was something else entirely to sleep without a fully locked door.

"Get some rest," Tina said. She walked into the hallway, and then she and Pete were gone.

Maggie stood in the darkness of the entryway. She closed the door and listened. There was the sound of Gerome's panting, the sound of Tina's and Pete's ascending footsteps in the stairwell, the sound of her own breathing. But that was it.

Mark came up behind her. He reached around her to lock, unlock, and relock the door. "Old school," he said. "I like it."

Without turning toward him, she reached for the doorknob and pulled. The door opened three inches before the lock caught. "You like this?" she said. She wedged her hand through the narrow opening. Her knuckles scuffed against the edge of the door's molding. "It still opens."

"I'll take my chances with the person who can slip through that crack," he said.

He brought her hand in from the other side and shut the door.

"Maggie," he said. He took her by the shoulders and rotated her so that she was facing him, though eye contact was impossible in the darkness. Gerome was still on his leash, still at their sides. He was whining.

"Maggie," Mark said again. "It's going to be all right." He kissed her on her forehead. They both smelled of sweat. "Hold out your hand."

She held out her hand. He took a glow stick from his pocket, snapped it, then tied it to her wrist. "See?" he said. "Now you're bona fide."

She looked down.

"Bona fide what?" she said.

"Bona fide country."

"And then some," she said.

All she needed to do was relax. Relax and let him be the man.

From the Sumerians, a 5,000-year-old society, we receive the word *love* as a compound verb. At the time and taken literally, this word — this *love* — meant the measuring of the earth or the demarcation of the land. Love, in other words, was a business, and its business meant marriage, and marriage meant the maintenance, the preservation, the endurance of society.

Mark bent down and unhooked Gerome, who stretched out and down on his forearms, then shook his whole body dramatically — a simple but instinctive display of freedom.

"That's it," said Mark. "Shake the human off." He reached down and took Maggie's hand, and the two of them stood like that — hand in hand, glow stick next to glow stick — listening as their dog moved from corner to corner of the room, sniffing, exploring, familiarizing himself with their temporary retreat.

21

It was twenty minutes before Gerome calmed down. He whined, panted, whined some more. Maggie kept letting him up on the bed, which Mark wouldn't have minded if there hadn't been another perfectly good bed for the dog to sleep on all by himself and if it hadn't been ninety degrees inside, which it was.

While Maggie was babying Gerome, Mark worked on the windows. They were on the first floor and Maggie kept saying he shouldn't open them, that it wouldn't be safe; but he was suffocating from the heat. His skin — his palms, his fingers, his lower back, every inch of him — was clammy.

Finally he was able to jimmy open the window closest to the bed, and even Maggie, after biting her lip and wringing her hands, admitted that the breeze felt nice.

Gerome, of his own volition, jumped off their bed, drank some water, then jumped up on the other bed. Maggie stripped their mattress of everything but the sheets, and now — finally, blissfully, thankfully — they were both lying down.

The only light came from the glow sticks on Maggie's side of the bed. But even that meager glimmer was weakening. Soon it would be pure shadow in their room. Soon they would be asleep.

For a while Mark lay on his back listening to the noises, his eyes closed. From down the hallway, he thought he heard the sound of a faucet running. Soon after, he thought he heard water in the pipes.

Then it was quiet. Gerome had begun to snore, but Maggie's breathing was too regular and he knew she wasn't yet sleeping.

Outside, the sound of a diesel approached, slowed, and stopped. For many minutes, he listened to the gentle *puh-puh-puh* of its engine as it idled outside the hotel. He imagined other travelers, weary just as they had been, standing at the front desk, meeting Tina and Pete, being given the rehearsed terms of their potential night's rest: clean sheets, clean towels, cold running water, nothing more.

Several minutes after it arrived, the diesel moved away from them. *No dice*, Mark thought. The world turned up only so many suckers in one night.

Outside their first-floor window, beyond the hotel's parking lot, past its concrete margin, Mark imagined what was there: loblolly pines by the dozen, shortleaf and spruce like he couldn't believe; hemlock and basswood wedged for position next to hickory and beech; black cherry and white oak, silk grass and sugar maple; gorges and slopes lousy with flora, slippery and slimy with rainwater and soil. Probably, too — in the kingdom of Plantae, in the division of Magnoliophyta, in the family of Fabaceae — there was kudzu, palming the mountainside like a great green hand. Robert told Mark as a boy of its self-propagating runners that cartwheel from one root to the next — onward, outward, onward, outward — of its instinctive need for reproduction; its twirling vines, its twisting and twining tentacles. In a single day, kudzu can grow an entire foot. Imagine: half an inch in an hour; two-tenths of a millimeter in a minute; three-thousandths of the same in a second. Which meant that even now, even as Mark lay there in the dark, kudzu might be growing. In the shimmering slick darkness beyond their window, it might be expanding. This very moment, its grasp on the mountain could be tightening.

Mark rolled onto his side. He couldn't see Maggie's face, but he could see the white of her underpants. She was lying on her back, her breasts exposed to the air, her arms straight at her sides.

"You awake?" he said. He found that he was whispering. He found also that he was heroically and unexpectedly turned on.

There was no response.

"You aren't talking to me?"

"Mm."

"Are you giving me the silent treatment, or are you actually asleep?"

He scooted closer.

"Neither?" She said it like a question.

"You were right to make us stay," he said.

"I'm not so sure," she said. "Stubborn is as stubborn does."

In the dark like this, neither of them able to make eye contact even if they wanted, things felt good between them, things felt right. At least on Mark's end. He felt, at this moment, very much as if they were a team, as if that little hotel room and everything in it — him and Maggie, yes, but also the dog, the beds, the pillows, the sheets — they were all on a team, a team against the world. They were stranded together. Beached, marooned, abandoned, but also self-reliant. The natural accumulation of years together — years of contempt and contentment, disappointment and settlement, all of it — seemed to drift away on a tide of blackness.

He tried — only to see, only as a test — to summon his earlier vexation, his previous frustration, but he couldn't conjure it. He was aroused even more, aroused at his own lack of agitation.

"It's not like you to sleep without a top on," said Mark.

"Is that a remark?" She was also whispering. The bed rocked as she softly shifted onto her side to face him. The glow beyond her shoulder was nearly gone.

"Remark?"

He could smell her breath, feel it on his face, faint and warm.

"About my paranoia?"

He reached up, found her cheek, ran his thumb across her eyelid. "No," he said. "It's really not."

She inched toward him. He could feel it.

"Do you think you can sleep?" she said.

"Even if I can't, just lying down is good. Just lying in the dark feels good on my eyes."

"I can't even tell if my eyes are open or closed," she said.

He ran his thumb across her eyelid again. "Closed," he said.

They were quiet. He stroked her hair, but nothing more. Not yet.

After a while she spoke. "I know how to make you sleep."

"What do you know?" he said.

It was a routine.

It was a signal.

It was code, their code.

"I know what you like," she said.

"How do you know what I like?"

He moved his body closer.

"I know," she said.

"How?"

She inched closer still.

"I know you," she said.

"Do you?"

"Better than you think."

"Is that right?" he said.

He let his hand drift from her ear to her neck to her shoulder.

"And you know me," she said.

"Do I?"

His hand left her shoulder, traveled the length of her side, came to her thigh.

She emitted a tiny noise — half moan, half sigh.

"You do," she said.

They didn't talk anymore.

After, Maggie tiptoed slowly to the bathroom and Mark lay once again on his back, now with his arms behind his head, listening as Maggie felt her way across the unfamiliar room. He felt a knightly rush of life.

He listened to his dog snore. He listened to his wife pee, then flush. He listened to the water gurgle through the pipes in the walls around him. *Alive,* he thought. *Alive. Alive.*

Maggie crept back to the bed, climbed under the cheap top sheet.

She put a hand on his stomach. "Too hot for this?" she said.

"Not at all," he said.

She was asleep within seconds, her soft snore the wings of a moth against a glass pane.

In the middle of nowhere, he thought. *In the middle of nowhere, as it always should be.*

Thoreau would strip naked and walk into his pond, walk all the way out until only his nose and eyes were above the water. He'd stay this way for hours, watching the bugs that dart down and up, down and up atop the quiet surface. He remained so still and for so long that he became a part of nature. Still a man, but more than a man. A man connected to the visceral, the real, to the vegetation and wildlife of the world.

Mark hadn't written Elizabeth back the other day. He hadn't told her that, yes, in fact, Maggie *was* the love of his life. But he would. It would be his last letter to the West Coast, and he'd write it the first chance he got. Over and out, Elizabeth.

What it was — this feeling — what it was, was freedom. The *feeling* of freedom. Freedom from cities and from the grid. Freedom to walk without being seen, without being monitored, without monitoring. He felt he'd finally stripped naked, finally walked out into his own pond, finally connected with the realness of the world. It had to do with getting away from technology and getting back to nature. It had to do with a generosity of spirit. It had to do with keeping very, very quiet in the middle of nowhere.

22

Maggie was surprised to find herself thinking about sex. For so many months her fantasies had involved supermarkets and shopping malls — public, inappropriate spaces devoid of possible intimacy. Earlier on this very night, anticipating Mark's probable desires, she'd recoiled at the prospect of being asked to engage. But something about Tina and Pete — about their musky tenderness toward one another — had flipped a switch, and, as Mark fiddled with the window cranks, Maggie gradually became aware of that sublimely simple craving. She wanted to be touched. She longed to be caressed, squeezed, jostled into various and necessary positions.

The only problem was that she didn't want to ask or explain. She wanted Mark to read her, understand her the way beast understands beast. Forget words, forget language altogether. She wanted them to be wolves and let their bodies do the speaking.

She pulled off her shorts, took off her T-shirt, and unhooked her bra. Then she lay down on the bed and waited. The breeze prickled her skin.

It took Mark maybe five minutes to notice she was topless. After that, it took very little time or energy before they were having sex.

In the bathroom, after, Maggie ran her hands tentatively along the sink's counter, looking for the unopened pack of glow sticks. She didn't find them but knocked over what felt like a short stack of washcloths. They made a soft *thump* against the tile floor. Perhaps they'd already opened the last pack. She couldn't now recall.

One hand after the other, she fumbled her way to the toilet. The pattern of the tile felt foreign against the tips of her fingers. The toilet was a full foot left of where she remembered it being when Pete had quickly shone the flashlight around the bathroom's corners. She thought of Audrey Hepburn alone and blind, groping, unaware of the burglar so close at hand. She thought of Jodie Foster in that basement, the murderer mere inches from her outstretched hand. She thought again of the coed. Eventually she made contact with the toilet's tank.

She lifted the lid and then sat. The porcelain was cold. She wiped away the sex and peed.

She was aware of the knock of her heartbeat; aware of the splash of her urine hitting the water in the bowl beneath her. She wondered if anyone else in the hotel could hear. She was sure Mark could. She'd left the door open when she walked in, not wanting to be alone. But now she felt vulnerable.

She wiped again, felt until she found the handle, then flushed. The water gurgled beneath her. She stood, pulled up her underwear, but then sat immediately back down. She was overtaken by loneliness.

She knew better than to associate it with Mark specifically or even with her current and unpredictable state of mind more generally. There is a sadness after sex, always: the philosophers say so; the poets say so. And this, right now, was Maggie's own *bleak little minute of irrational sadness,* which was how Augustine had put it some sixteen hundred years ago. Some things never changed.

Maybe — *god* — maybe it wasn't loneliness or sadness at all. Maybe it was simply the quiet. She missed the buzz, the low steady *prrr* of electricity. This momentary excursion into the forlorn could be that simple. It could.

She put her elbows on her knees and her head in her hands.

The long and short of it, the plain and simple fact: Mark was afraid of technology and Maggie was afraid of people.

Her question: Could they move forward — together or alone — in a world filled with technology *and* people?

Were they already doomed? Or was tragedy behind them now for good? Maggie felt unsure of everything at that moment. Nice *tits* or nice *day?* She didn't know earlier and she didn't know now.

She leaned back against the toilet's tank. It felt cool and clean against her skin. She closed her eyes, opened them, closed them again. There was no difference. Black, black, black. It was a metaphor for something — for life maybe: it was the same whether you looked or didn't, the same whether you acknowledged the evil lurking in the corner or ignored it. If the plane's going down, the plane's going down. It doesn't matter how aggressively you grit your teeth, how hard you grip the armrests. The end is the end is the end, plain and simple. Maybe Mark was right about everything. Maybe he always had been.

She moved her hands from her thighs to her breasts, and now she held them — her right breast in her left hand and her left in her right. Their weight felt pleasant, if a little sweaty. Four-plus decades and they were still pretty good. The nipples, never having breastfed, were still capable of expanding and contracting. Just now they were hard, responding to her own touch. But later, asleep for a few hours next to her husband, they would expand, flatten, turn round and light in color.

She stood up, a flutter of lightness in her chest.

Something else Augustine had said? That a woman's caress served only to bring down a man's mind. It wasn't verbatim, of course. But the point was, screw Augustine! Screw bleakness, irrational or otherwise!

Maggie didn't need to be sad if she didn't want to be. This weight she'd been carrying around hadn't paid any real homage to the coed; it had only served to suck the life out of her marriage. That man out there — *my man!* — was her husband, and Maggie's love, physical or otherwise, didn't lower him; it elevated him. Just as his did her.

The point?

The point?

The point?

To hell with the poets. To hell with the coed. This was *her* life, not theirs.

23

Mark slept. It was a shallow sleep. He was aware of his breathing. He was aware of outside sounds. At some point he had a dream in which Maggie, at too great a distance from him to be saved, was drowning. She was wailing. *Mlip, mlip, mlip.* She sobbed as the water went in and out of her mouth, as her arms flailed and snot collected in her nose. *Mlip, mlip, mlip.*

When the sound finally woke him, and eventually it had to, Mark discovered that it wasn't from within but from without. It was Gerome, whining again. He was standing at their bed, at Mark's side of their bed, his chin smashed against the mattress, and he was whining.

"Get in your bed," Mark whispered. "Get in your bed." It was a command Gerome knew by heart.

But the dog didn't get in his bed. Instead, he continued to whine. He pawed at the mattress. This wasn't like him.

"Fuck," he said.

Gerome pawed more frantically now at the sheets. There was no way to avoid getting out of bed, putting on his pants and shoes, groping his way out of the building, and waiting while the dog did his business.

Mark threw off the top sheet.

It would be sunup soon. For now, though, the room was still dark, and Mark searched his way over to the armchair where he'd tossed his clothes only an hour or two earlier. He pulled on his shirt, which was stiff from the dried rain, then stepped into his pants. The legs were still wet.

Gerome came to him, leaned into his shins. He was whimpering now, a way of apologizing for the inconvenience. Gerome hated this as much as Mark did. He was embarrassed — embarrassed by his animal nature; embarrassed he couldn't express himself clearly through words; embarrassed that what was happening in his body was beyond his control. Poor dog. It wasn't right that he would be ashamed of himself. He was just being himself, a dog being a dog.

In an undergraduate honors seminar, Mark had a student, just this last semester, who'd insisted, in front of the entire class, that *to equivocate* was the same as *to equate*. Mark had had to stop the discussion in order to correct the mistake. It wasn't that he wanted to humiliate the undergrad; rather, he wanted to avoid other students' adoption of the misunderstanding. What had surprised Mark, more than anything else, was the kid's unwillingness to surrender his belief. Even after Mark had explained — at length, using the whiteboard — the immense difference between the two words, the student had insisted on his own accuracy. There was, Mark had begun to understand that day, a fundamental difference between this upcoming generation and all the ones that had come before. It was the absence of humility, the inability to admit defeat, the unwillingness to be wrong. *Be wrong,* he thought standing in front of his class. *Just be wrong.* What ʰought now was that Gerome, though he couldn't know it, was blessed with something essential, something that no amount of training or housebreaking could ever fully eliminate: animal instinct. Whereas, it seemed, on the contrary, that man was capable — more and more — of losing humanity. Every year, the students in Mark's classroom were less and less human. Every year, there was something *essential* missing.

In Mark's front pocket was the last packet of glow sticks. He tore it open, pulled out all three sticks, snapped each one, and tied them to his wrist. The room immediately around him came into pastel view. Gerome wagged his tail and circled.

"Where's your leash?" Mark whispered. "Where'd it go?"

Gerome ran to the door and nosed at the place where they'd discarded the leash.

"Good boy," Mark said.

Once the dog's collar was hooked, Mark eeked open the high-levered lock. It was only after he was in the hallway shutting the door carefully and quietly that he realized he'd be leaving Maggie in an unlocked room. He paused. The hallway was so black; he didn't like the idea of leaving Maggie exposed.

Gerome let out a full-mouthed moan at his side. Mark saw no other option. He pulled the door closed. It didn't latch. But, provided no one came through checking, it would appear, were there light, as though the door was flush with the frame. It was the best he could do.

Gerome tugged him down the hall, past the fire door, through the lower stairwell, and out the basement exit. Outside, the air was dank and fluid. His moist pants felt cool against his legs.

There was a minivan parked near the rear exit of the hotel. Gerome steered deftly around it, leading them rapidly across the bottom parking lot in the direction of the forest at the perimeter of the clearing.

Two more cars were parked in the distance, near the far edge of the mountaintop — a low sedan and a high-riding truck. Neither of them had their headlights on, but one of them — one of the far ones — was idling. Or Mark thought it was idling. He thought he could hear the engine gently ticking in the distance. Maybe he was imagining things. Maybe what he was actually hearing was the beginning of the return of electricity, its whirs and hums.

Gerome hunched into a squat the minute he hit grass and relieved himself. The smell was foul. He crab-walked along the edge of the trees, through the sodden grass, in the direction of the far cars. Mark breathed shallowly through his mouth and followed, the leash taut and his arm outstretched in order to provide as much distance between them as possible.

The earliest smidgen of light was visible to the east. Mark rubbed at his eyes. At long last, Gerome stopped, shook himself frantically, then returned daintily to Mark's side, his tail high, as though nothing had ever been troubling him.

There was just enough residual moon and just enough burgeoning morning sun that Mark could see now that the truck, definitely idling, had a door open. In fact, from its massive outline, it looked not unlike the truck they'd been followed by a few hours earlier.

Mark stepped closer.

Above the purr of the engine — impossible, of course — but above the purr, he thought he heard a whimper. Then the noise, the one that sounded like a whimper, morphed — further impossible — into a sob, and the sob into a word, and the word — the one Mark heard — was *no*, and the *no* seemed very much as if it were being uttered by a woman.

A moment later there was a slap — what sounded like a slap — and this was then followed by a full-on cry.

But the cry didn't belong to a woman. It belonged to a child.

Instinctively, Mark craned his head, his better ear angled more directly toward the vehicles.

The woman's voice, higher, clearer, now said, "Stop." There was another slap.

It was impossible — these sounds, this series of sounds — because things like this didn't happen in real life. Not to Mark. Things like this happened on TV, on scripted police procedurals, in Maggie's articles. They didn't happen to him.

There was another sharp cry — the child again — and then what could only be described as a gasping, as though something were drowning or possibly being smothered.

Gerome lifted his head as if to say, *It's not just you, bub. It's you and me both, and you know a dog has ears designed to detect distress. You know it, bub. There's no denying it. Try all you want.*

Mark felt his pulse pick up. The question, of course, was whether to approach or retreat. The options were to go back to the hotel room and pretend he'd heard nothing, or advance toward the car and risk giving the impression of a classic busybody.

He thought of Maggie, of what she'd do, what she'd say. "If you see something, say something," she might quip. "Do you want to be polite, or do you want to be proactive?" He thought of the college girl.

Gerome tugged in the direction of the two vehicles. The little bell on his collar jingled. Mark yanked him back. He yelped. "Quiet," he said. "Quiet."

The sun was up a degree higher, though it was still closer to night than to day. He could see the color of Gerome's fur. In another few minutes, he'd be able to see the make of the two vehicles in front of them. In a few minutes after that, he'd see their license plates. In a few minutes more, he'd see into the windshields. But he didn't want to see into the windshields. He didn't want to see the numbers on the plates, and he surely didn't want to engage with anybody who might have been following them so belligerently just a few hours earlier on that slim mountain road.

He turned toward the hotel — he'd made his decision — but it was too late: Mark and Gerome had been spotted.

"Hey," said a voice from inside the opened door of the truck. This was a man's voice, not a woman's, not a child's. Perhaps Mark had been mistaken. Perhaps both he and Gerome had been mistaken. "Wait a minute," the voice said.

Mark's cheeks went hot. He'd been caught meddling. His bowels churned loudly.

A figure now emerged from the truck, the outline of a man, of a very large man. Mark thought he heard the sound of a zipper. He felt sick.

The figure stepped forward; Gerome growled, and Mark heard the unmistakably muffled mewl of a child coming from within the truck. Mark backed up.

"You need something?" the man said. His voice was familiar — not associated with a singular person, but with a specific *type* of person, with a specific *breed*. In his voice was the twang of mountains, the thud of poverty, the absence of education, the clash of inbreeding.

The man stopped walking when Gerome growled again.

"Pete?" said Mark. "Is that you?"

"Who's Pete? I'm not Pete. You want something?"

"Who do you have in there?"

"You work here? You asking me to leave?"

Mark heard rustling from the interior of the truck. Something was wrong. A struggle was underway. He was sure of it.

"Do you have permission to be here?" Mark asked. "Who do you have in there?"

"Are you the person who gives permission?" the man said. "Is that for you to give?"

The rustling continued.

"Does someone need help?" It was the only thing Mark could think to ask, though having asked it, he realized how weak the question sounded, how ineffectual and insincere even.

And now, inside the truck, an overhead light flicked on. A young woman uncrumpled herself from the passenger's seat. Her hair was disheveled; she appeared half asleep. Her face, what Mark could see through the windshield, was pale blue and hollow.

He heard the mewling again. And then, against his will, though will had nothing to do with it since he'd not been prepared or forewarned, he watched as the woman pulled aside her shirt and exposed a breast.

Mark looked away and toward the man, who was looking now at what Mark had just seen. The man stepped sideways, a defensive move, meant to block Mark's view. The maneuver worked, but not before Mark looked once again — this time, yes, against his will; it was instinct; it was animal; he shouldn't have but he did — toward the breast and saw, just before the vision was interrupted by the shadow of the man, a baby being lifted up from the deep of the cab, up and toward the breast.

"Who needs help?" asked the man. "You need help? You got extra food lying around? Water? You want to give me something? Maybe you want to give my wife something?" The man spit. The *thwack* against the pavement was indisputable. "We're not that sort of people."

The man stepped forward. Mark stepped back.

"You want to fuck with my family?"

Gerome growled, but the man now didn't retreat.

Mark was shaking his head while backing away. It was a second or two before he realized a verbal response was in order. He thought he might puke.

"No," he said. "No. Just walking the dog. I'm sorry."

He held up the leash, stupidly. He couldn't yet make out the face of the man across from him. He didn't want to. He was thankful for shadows.

The light inside the truck clicked off. The passenger door opened. The woman stepped down. It appeared that the baby was still attached, still suckling. "You some sort of perv?" The woman was talking to Mark. The question was outrageous.

Now the woman joined her husband, a unified front. "He some sort of perv?" she said to the man. She let the word linger too long in her mouth — *prrrrrv* — giving it more space, more time, more cadence than it deserved; giving it time to latch on as a possibly accurate descriptor.

"You want me to wake the others?" She was talking to her husband, whispering in fact, but Mark heard her plain and clear. *Others.*

"Sure," she said, no response one way or another from the man she stood beside, the man who seemed nearly statuesque in his determination and surveillance of Mark.

"Sure," said the woman. "Sure, sure. I'm waking them." The baby still latched to her chest, she moved toward the sedan.

"It's nothing," said Mark. He shrugged his shoulders, a lame attempt to look meek, repentant. He turned again toward the hotel. He tested taking one, then another, step away.

The man said, "Hey."

Mark kept walking.

He heard what sounded like a knock on a window. A car door opened, maybe two car doors.

Again the man said, "Hey."

But Mark didn't stop; wouldn't stop. His heartbeat raced violently.

Behind him, there was more whispering. Mark couldn't make out the words — he was too far now or the words were too low — but as he continued his escape, he believed he could detect different tones, various octaves. How many people were back there? How many women? How many babies? Oh god, he wondered, how many men?

Mark was halfway across the parking lot — an even distance between himself, the hotel, the bank of trees, and the offending automobiles — when he and Gerome were suddenly awash in a bath of headlights. He turned. Both the truck and the sedan beside it had turned on their high beams.

An engine revved. Gerome bolted.

Mark faltered, tripping over his own foot with the other. He tried to recover but lost his grip on the leash. Gerome sprinted toward the tree line. Mark called his name, but the dog continued his flight.

The sedan and the truck pulled forward in unison. Mark watched the dog's outline. He ran first for the woods then halted midcourse. Mark called his name again: "Gerome!" The dog turned, paused, then made a beeline not toward Mark but toward the hotel.

He ran in and out of the headlights of the sedan. His brilliant brown coat was lit up momentarily.

The sedan swerved toward the rear exit of the parking lot, and Gerome swerved too. He went dark, but only for a second. Mark could hear his collar ringing, heading again for the forest.

Gerome appeared once more, now in the headlights of the truck, which was moving too fast around the far side of the hotel. He was midair, all four feet aloft in a magnificent leap toward the grass. A single bound separated him from asphalt and the trees.

The truck, unlike the sedan, didn't swerve, and the sound — the terrible *whump* followed by his dog's pitiful cry — sent Mark running.

The truck didn't stop, and in the distance he was aware of the drowning sound of two cars speeding haphazardly away.

Gerome had landed with his body on the pavement and his head, resting almost gingerly, on the concrete lip of the parking lot.

Mark tried to get him to stand, but he wouldn't obey. He would only moan.

Then Mark tried to pick him up, but each attempt, every maneuver, seemed to increase the dog's pain.

"Gerome, Gerome," he kept saying, as if in repetition a solution might be found. "Gerome, Gerome."

The sun in the east inched up from the earth.

The only answer was to bring Maggie outside, which meant leaving Gerome alone.

Mark looked around. Objects — trees, streetlamps, the hotel itself — had outlines, but none of the outlines was a person. There was no one to help him, no one to go for help for him.

"Stay here," he whispered to Gerome. "Stay here."

The dog groaned.

There was just enough light, just enough morning sun for Mark to see into the dog's eyes. He did something Maggie was always telling him to do, something he'd never before dignified by trying, but that now made perfect sense. He visualized the image of himself — *The Grown Man Inside! The Man Already a Man! It all had a purpose; everything had a purpose!* How had he never made the connection before? — running toward the hotel, waking Maggie, bringing her back to Gerome's side. He visualized the three of them together, happy, healthy, sound. He gave the image to Gerome. Through ether, through embers and fibers and neurons, through elements and atoms and strands, through filaments and particles and the universe itself, he sent the image from his brain to Gerome's.

"Do you understand?" he said. "Can you see it?"

Before the dog could answer, Mark, the man, was running.

24

It took her a minute before she remembered where they were, why they were there. Mark was yelling at her, but she didn't know why. He'd forced her into a seated position on the bed. He'd manipulated her legs so that her feet were touching the floor.

"Where's Gerome?" she said. Her mouth was sour. Her lower back was sore.

"That's what I'm telling you," he said. "He's been hit. Get up. Get out of bed."

Mark was handing her things, pieces of clothing. He was trying to force a damp shirt over her head. She pushed him away.

"What are you doing?" she said. "Get off. What are you doing?"

"Get out of bed," he said. "Get up. Come outside."

"Why is Gerome outside?" she asked. She pulled on her T-shirt and stood. Her knees cracked.

Before she could look for them, Mark had placed her shorts in her hands. They too were damp, and she pulled them on slowly. Her legs were wobbly, as though maybe they were still asleep.

"You left him outside alone?" she said. It didn't make sense. "Is he in the car? Did you leave the a/c running?"

"Please," said Mark. He was pulling her. He had taken her by the wrist, and now he was pulling her.

"My shoes," she said. "Do you have my shoes?" Her shorts weren't yet buttoned. She couldn't see where she was going. She took a step forward and ran into something hard with her toe. "Fuck," she said.

"I have your shoes," he said. "But please, Maggie. I need you to wake up. I need you to concentrate."

She was trying to take her shoes from his hands. He seemed unwilling to give them to her. Her toe was in exquisite agony. She sat back down on the bed.

"Maggie," he said.

She closed her eyes. It felt so good to close her eyes. She couldn't remember the last time she'd slept so soundly, so peacefully.

Mark slapped her.

She yelped.

Her eyes were open again.

"I'm sorry," Mark said. He was kneeling down in front of her now. "Are you listening?" He was rubbing both her knees with his hands. "Can you hear me?"

Her cheek was on fire.

"Maggie?"

She stood, slipped on her shoes, and pushed past Mark.

All at once she understood. All at once the last two minutes came into focus. It was as if she'd lived there her whole life, the way she pivoted the turns in the dark, the way she maneuvered the corners so effortlessly.

She was out of the room, out of the hallway, out of the hotel in an instant.

176

25

A violent fuchsia sun was just visible at the tip of the trees to the east.

Daybreak, at last.

The asphalt of the parking lot was wet. Lavender steam rose up in pockets around them like ghostly bouquets. Gerome was on his side, his head in Maggie's lap.

She was doing something with her hands, running them up and down his body. Any other day, any other setting, and this might have seemed normal. Just his wife giving the family dog a little shoulder massage while he slept. Mark wished they were back home, back in their apartment, in Chicago. He wished the asphalt was their Oriental rug and the hotel was just a wall. He wished the minivan was their sofa, and he wished what Maggie was saying right now was, "Bring me some coffee, will you? I don't want to disturb Gerome while he's sleeping so peacefully."

But that's not what she was saying. And the would-be urban setting of his imagination fell away, and he was back again squarely and cruelly in a parking lot at daybreak, his wife yelling up at him. "In the car," she was saying. "In the glove compartment. Get me my kit." He didn't know why he wasn't moving, but he wasn't. Not yet. "Mark," she said. "Goddamn it." She smacked him in the calf. "Get my kit. Do it now." Her other hand was still on Gerome, still performing some terribly clinical massage. The dog yapped and opened his eyes. They gazed upward at Mark. The look of confusion was galling. "Go," said Maggie again, and now Mark did go. He ran to their car, unlocked the passenger side, swept the contents of the glove compartment to the floor, and picked out the medical kit. Had he known such a thing existed? Had he known that Maggie kept it there? But when had she put it there? And when, before putting it there, had she taken the time to put the kit together? There was so much he hadn't thought of, so much he hadn't taken into account.

He ran back to Maggie. Her right hand was stationary, pressing hard on the dog's side.

"What now?" said Mark. "Tell me what to do."

"In the side pocket," she said. "The one with the zipper." She looked up. "Yes, that one. There are two needles. Do you see?"

He unzipped the little side pocket. "There's no blood," he said. "That's good, right? He's in shock, right? That's it?"

Maggie ignored him.

"Read the baggies," she said. "Do you see the one that says Telazol?"

Mark held out one of the needles. He was somehow unable to read what it said.

"Not that one," she said. "The other one. Hold it up for me."

He held out the second needle.

"Yes, okay. Good."

Gerome had started to pant. She leaned down and put her mouth to the dog's ear. Mark couldn't hear what she was saying. With her left hand she was stroking Gerome's neck.

She sat up again and looked at Mark. "Open the package for me. I can't do it with one hand."

"You need this?"

"Open it."

Mark opened it and held out the needle.

"What does it do?" he said. "Will it calm him down?"

Maggie took the needle.

"Good boy," she said. With her free thumb, she rubbed at a spot on his front leg. "Good boy."

She looked up at Mark. "Kneel down."

Mark knelt down.

"Put your hand here."

"Here?"

"Just there. That's right. Just how my hand is."

Mark did as he was told. The skin was hot and he felt — *oh god* — what did he feel? What was that protrusion under his dog's skin? He looked at Maggie.

"He's bleeding internally," she said. She was so calm. She was so matter-of-fact. "Do you understand?"

Mark could feel the lump beneath his hand. Was it getting hotter? Was it growing?

"No," he said. "I don't think I understand."

Maggie nodded. Her thumb was still rubbing at a place just behind Gerome's elbow. "I'm going to give him this shot. It will calm him. Like you said."

Mark found that he was nodding in time with Maggie, two metronomes perfectly in sync, though he felt several measures behind.

"Just to calm him," Mark said.

"And to take him out of pain."

"Good, good," said Mark. "Good. Yes. Do it."

"Are you still pressing? The pressure helps take away the pain too."

"I'm pressing." And he was pressing, and what he was pressing into felt like it was pressing back. "I think I can feel the leak," he said. "I think it's right here. Is that good? What happens next?"

Maggie's head was bowed in concentration. She pushed the needle into Gerome's arm, where her thumb had been. Slowly, she pressed the plunger until the top was flush with the barrel. Gerome let out a little sigh. Maggie set the syringe down. She stroked the dog's ears. "That's better," she said. "That's better."

Now she reached for the kit and from it removed the second syringe.

"What's that?" Mark said. "What are you doing now?"

Maggie looked at him. Had she been crying the entire time? It seemed to him that she hadn't been crying before. Only now she was. Now that things were better, that Gerome was beyond danger and out of pain.

"Mark," she said, tearing at the package with her teeth. "This will happen fast. Okay? This will happen very quickly."

Mark was shaking his head now. "What are you talking about? What are you doing? He's fine."

"He's not fine." She was rubbing him again, awful circular motions, only now she was rubbing the spot above his heart. A little sniffling sound came from somewhere on her face. "He's bleeding internally. There's nothing I can do. There's nothing either of us can do."

She moved her hand from Gerome's shoulder to Mark's fingers. She squeezed them just slightly. "This isn't anyone's fault. Even if we were in a hospital right now, this would be the only option." Now she had her hand fully on top of Mark's, the one that had been pressing so purposefully on Gerome's side. She squeezed again. "You can let go," she said. "Love, you can let go."

But he didn't want to let go. He didn't want it to end this way. This wasn't right. He wanted her to fix him. He wanted her to make it better. He wanted to feel that strong heartbeat, which he realized now, beneath his open palm, had slowed considerably.

"Come around here," she said. "Come here. Come be by me. Come talk to him. Let him know it's okay."

She pulled at Mark gently. He obeyed.

"When I put this needle in, when the liquid is gone, it will happen fast," she said.

Mark cupped his hand around the dog's ear.

"Nod so I know you understand," she said.

He nodded.

"This one goes into his heart. It sounds painful, but it won't be. He's sleeping already. You see? So this needle goes in and then it takes fifteen seconds, that's it." She spoke deliberately, evenly. It was possible she didn't know she was crying.

She put her left hand on Mark's again and then around and under Gerome's neck. She raised herself onto a knee and, with her right hand, guided the needle into the spot above Gerome's heart.

The plunger moved down the barrel.

The liquid disappeared.

Maggie removed the needle.

All at once, she gasped, then threw the needle aside. She put her hands suddenly to her face and slumped into a little heap at Gerome's side.

Mark sat there, helpless.

26

It was fully light out now. Still morning, but light out. The hotel was an ugly double-decker affair made of cinder blocks and brick. It was situated on a small hill, in what appeared to be some sort of office park, a vestige from a time when the town believed it was capable of more. But it was just a foolish little mountain town; there was nothing any more or less special about its views and streams or rocks and pebbles than any other piddly municipality in West Virginia in the middle of nowhere. No, there was nothing special or frightening or interesting at all about Black Crows Hill, except this was where their dog had died. How stupid.

Maggie took a sheet from their hotel room, which, in the light of day, was nondescript and mockingly harmless. She went out the back way but not because she cared about the petite clerk girl or her oafish boyfriend and what they might say. They could charge her double, triple.

She was careful not to let the sheet drag along the parking lot. She wanted it clean for Gerome. He would have liked that it had her smell on it — her smell and Mark's — even from a few hours' worth of sleep.

Just as she wasn't worried about what Tina or Pete might say if she'd been caught taking the sheet, neither was she worried about the fabric of the car. As she made a bed in the backseat with the sheet, she wasn't thinking about the leather, she was thinking about Gerome. It wasn't a matter of comfort at this point — he was dead, there was no changing that — but there was the matter of respect: respect for his body, respect for what he had been to them. A constant. An old pal. A faithful trouper. A total Loyalist.

Using the front and back headrests, she created a sort of hammock out of the sheet, which she imagined — if Gerome were still alive — would have felt to him like some wonderful hug all along his body. She was aware, as she tested to make sure the sheet would stay in place, of Mark watching. She wasn't angry with him. She'd meant it when she said it wasn't his fault. Things would be difficult for a while. She knew that. He'd blame himself even if she didn't. But something good would come of all this. Even if she had to root around in filth and muck, she would find the goodness. She owed it to Gerome. She would be better, calmer. She would pick up more hours at the clinic — they'd name one of the rooms after Gerome, in his memory. She'd get back to the gym. She'd take up cooking again. Hadn't she once loved to cook dinner for Mark? Starting in Virginia, starting with these couple months at the farm with Mark's parents, she'd give up the Internet. Yes. This was the place to start. She'd give up the Internet, and she'd find polite ways to get out of watching the morning news with Robert. She'd do some gardening with Gwen. Plus there were the horses and golf. She'd do all this, and Mark would be buoyed by her pluck.

She couldn't yet think about the return drive home, but once back in Chicago she would get rid of every hidden stash of pills, every hoard of would-be weaponry. She blushed just thinking about all the hiding places — the can of mace at the bottom of the toilet paper basket, the little contraband switchblade in the silverware drawer that she'd ordered off eBay and had shipped to the clinic. It was almost funny how quickly things were coming into view — how she could suddenly see so clearly just how fearfully she'd been living. The fact of the matter: Maggie wasn't the coed and the coed wasn't Maggie. Two different men, two different crimes, two different women, two different outcomes. It was all a matter of luck, life was. You could beg all you wanted for protection, you could pray or not pray to a god or to a devil, but what it all came down to was a simple game of chance.

When Maggie was satisfied that the hammock would hold, and after she'd tucked and retucked the sheet in all the right places, she turned to Mark.

"Do you think you can pick him up?"

He nodded.

"I'll help situate him from the other side," she said.

Mark bent down in front of Gerome. For a moment, he just knelt there, his fingers resting on the dog's muzzle. Then he pushed his hands under the dog's back and scooted him into the crook of his arms with a gentle bounce. He stood up slowly. He was being so careful. Maggie felt grateful for him just then, grateful that there was someone else who cared as much as she.

"Are you ready?" she said.

Mark was at the car, Gerome still balanced perfectly in his arms. One day — it was too soon to think about now — but one day there would be another dog. There had to be.

Mark nodded again, and together — as softly as they could — they installed Gerome in the backseat.

To anyone looking down, looking in, the sheet might have seemed a simple dog bed, and Gerome just a sleeping dog, waiting to get where his owners were going.

27

Maggie took the driver's seat. Mark didn't argue. From somewhere in the hotel she'd procured a small map of the Virginias. She folded it open to the appropriate section and drove them expertly down and out of the mountain and back to 64.

A plump sun was firmly in the sky by the time they reentered the highway. The big rigs were already on the road. The day was fully underway. Mark would never tell her about the truck or the sedan, what he'd seen, how it had happened. He would never mention that sickly swollen breast, the man who feared Mark a predator, the family — families? — too poor to pay for a hotel. *You some sort of perv?* The question had hit him like a fist to the gut. Unintentionally — oh, how this would have disappointed Maggie! — he had stepped into the role of villain. It didn't matter that he'd been equally frightened by them. They couldn't sense his fear. "People don't seem to mind their business like they used to." Maggie had said so just the day before! And now he'd gone and invaded another family's space; treated the parking lot as an extension of his own property; challenged another's right to exist. His motivations might have been pure, but his actions — at least as perceived by that man, that woman, whoever else was camping out there with them — were entirely intrusive. In trying to be useful, Mark had overstepped; in overstepping, he'd ended their dog's life. He shuddered to think where those people might be now: huddled and hungry and scared, no doubt, in the cramped compartments of their too-hot automobiles.

Maggie turned on the radio and rolled down the windows. Gerome didn't yet smell, but soon he would. Before they reached the farm, there would be an odor, but the would-be odor was the least of their woes.

The talk on the radio was all about the storm, about its aftermath. Dozens of cities were without power, thousands of people were dangerously low on potable water, hundreds of homes had been destroyed. It was unclear how many had died. The deejay sounded jazzed, not saddened by the possibility that the number might be severe. Politicians were continuing to weigh in. They were already thinking about the next election.

Except for the people they'd impacted, Katrina had been forgotten, Sandy had been forgotten, and this storm too would eventually be forgotten. Next month a new horror story would unfold and the month after that a newer one. Next winter there'd be a typhoon and the summer following there would be an earthquake. After that, a tsunami would hit.

Just recently a pal at Penn had conducted a study about violence in movies and the tenuous nature of the MPAA's rating system. In only fifteen minutes, during which time hundreds of bloody clips out of context were shown, parents had gone from being outraged by the cruelty to being irked to being indifferent. Fifteen minutes.

Humans — every single one of them — would become more and more immune to the news. Soon they would be able to watch a beheading without flinching. Mark could see the future clear as day. The world, and Maggie, and one day even he would lose the ability to be horrified.

Evil — sometimes anonymous, sometimes known — not only existed, it thrived. It was in their neighborhood in Chicago, and it was at the gas station outside Indianapolis, and according to that family in the parking lot, it was there inside him too, which meant it was everywhere. The Internet would continue and technology would advance. It was just a matter of time. They were all headed in the same downward direction. There was no generosity of spirit. It had been bred out. Just look at Mark. The slap he'd supposedly heard, those words — "stop," "no" — they had existed without context. It was Mark who'd filled in the dirty explanation as it suited him. Where was his generosity? Gone. He'd used his biased imagination to color in the missing pieces: they were poor; they were inbred, so necessarily there was abuse, neglect.

Do you think, Maggie had asked not twenty-four hours earlier, *that you willfully see the worst in people?*

His honest answer: Not willfully. But accidentally — perhaps intuitively — yes, he did. He understood that now.

Take away technology, and evil would still be there because goodness had evaporated. Mark and Maggie could recite poetry all they wanted, but the shepherd boy was dead. Elizabeth's egoism — her privilege, her cockiness — it wasn't valiant. It was churlish. And he'd been naïve to be attracted to it in the first place. This was the true condition of man — *nasty, brutish, and short.*

At least he had Maggie. That's one thing he felt sure of. Another? That she'd been right all along: People were shit, including him. They were all on the decline, a steep and fast decline. But they — he and Maggie — were on it together, battling the storm in the same defenseless boat. They had no chance of defeating it, of course. But they could try. From Maggie, he could learn to be better. Realizing his complacency was the first step.

Except . . .

If nothing was permanent . . .

If everything ended . . .

Then mightn't this current trend end as well? Wasn't there the possibility that they could wait it out? Noah waited out the flood, didn't he? Or so the story went, which was all that mattered — the stories people told, because it was from the stories that they learned; it was in the past that they saw the future. Wasn't there the very likely prospect that people would one day — perhaps even soon — tire of the constant noise, the tell-all blogs, the endless media rotations?

They passed a sign for Beckley. Soon, their car would cross the state line. They were less than two hundred miles from Charlottesville. They would be able to bury Gerome before rigor mortis set in. In an hour or so, when they stopped for gas, Mark would get out his phone and call his mother. He'd do it while Maggie was in the bathroom so that she wouldn't have to hear the banal specifics of the conversation. He'd tell her the gist of what had happened. He'd keep it brief, straightforward. He'd have Gwen instruct Robert to get to work on a grave; they'd probably need to get the backhoe out in order for the hole to be deep enough. He'd tell her to have him dig it in the shade garden, under the rope swing, where Gerome preferred to spend his afternoons. They'd bury him with a few of his favorite toys — his grasshopper, his rabbit. But he'd caution Gwen and Robert from being overly maudlin. Maggie wouldn't like it. They'd give her space, as much space as she needed.

He leaned his head back against the leather. Only a few hours earlier, they'd made love. He and his wife. He and his Maggie. They hadn't used a condom. Normally they were so careful. Had she forgotten intentionally? Had he? He sat up a little. *Good god,* he thought. *What if?* He couldn't remember the last time he'd entertained a new idea so cleanly. Like a pebble in his mouth, he moved the idea around, getting to know its unfamiliar edges and lines, its bends and curves.

He tried to imagine the next few weeks. He tried to imagine not the imminent burial but the days afterward: meals he'd cook with his mother; the inevitable talks with his father about the state of the university; drives through the country he'd take with Maggie. He'd fill a cooler with a six-pack of Mexican beer and a sliced-up lime, and they'd drink and drive on the private roads the way Maggie always liked.

And maybe — who knows? — he'd go ahead and broach the subject, the possibility. He'd say, "Even if it doesn't happen now, accidentally, maybe we should think about doing it deliberately. What do you think?"

He imagined all the ways — so many, so easily — he could become (*and would!*) a better husband, a better son, and, perhaps, a better person. There would be fewer things to regret in the future, because there would be fewer mistakes.

He looked at Maggie, at her fine tight skin, her patrician jaw. They weren't too old. They really weren't. Not yet. He glanced down at her shirt, just below her breasts. Maybe (*Ludicrous! But maybe!*) there was a little human in there — well, a microscopic egg, not yet a human — but maybe there was an egg, and maybe that egg had been fertilized by a sperm and morphed into a zygote. Maybe even now her body was transforming. *Goddamn!* Everything really could serve a purpose. It *could*: the world could right itself; the decline could plateau then twist and rise; and Mark could believe: inside, somewhere hidden in Maggie's womb, waiting, not yet known, not yet knowable, there was a baby and a change and a chance for a different future. It was possible.

Anything is possible.

NOTES

The offered definition of *auto* is an amalgamation of entries culled from the *Oxford English Dictionary, Merriam-Webster*, and Apple's Dashboard Dictionary application.

The translation of Homer in the epigraph is my own. (Thanks, St. John's College!)

The following is a list of endlessly useful articles and books on which I relied to learn about everything from cloud factories to tornadoes:

"Auditory Brain Development in Premature Infants: The Importance of Early Experience," by Erin McMahon, Pia Wintermark, and Amir Lahav, published in *Annals of the New York Academy of Sciences*, April 2012.

"Into the Tornado," one of Discovery Channel's *Storm Chasers* videos, featuring Reed Timmer.

"The Cloud Factories: Power, Pollution and the Internet," by James Glanz, published in the *New York Times*, September 22, 2012.

Freaks of the Storm: From Flying Cows to Stealing Thunder: The

World's Strangest True Weather Stories, by Randy Cerveny (New York: Basic Books, 2005).

The Riso-Hudson Enneagram Type Indicator, http://www.enn eagraminstitute.com/.

"Parental Desensitization to Violence and Sex in Movies," a study conducted by the Annenberg Center for Public Policy at the University of Pennsylvania, *Pediatrics* 134, no. 5 (2014).

Handbook to Life in Ancient Mesopotamia, by Stephen Bertman (Oxford: Oxford University Press, 2005).

Maggie and Mark take liberties throughout, quoting (and misquoting) the following writers:

Wordsworth (specifically, "Ode: Intimations of Immortality from Recollections of Early Childhood")

St. Augustine ("the bleak little minute of irrational sadness")

Thomas Hobbes ("nasty, brutish, and short")

Arthur Schopenhauer ("Man can do what he wills but he cannot will what he wills" and "Hope is the confusion of the desire for a thing with its probability.")

THANKS TO

My dear friends Mark Rader and Maggie Vandermeer, who loaned me their perfect names

Ben Warner, who has now read every novel I've written — good or bad — and has advised me honestly throughout

Andrew Ewell, my husband, for his epic advice and constant confidence

Helen Atsma, for bringing this novel to life

Maria Massie, for shepherding it to its final home

Everyone who has ever encouraged me (the list is long, but you know who you are)

Bookstores and booksellers everywhere (this list is longer)

And, finally, you — the reader: thank you for reading . . .

08/09/14